PRAISE FOR
A CONVENIENT HEART

"My fellow readers, so I will just say that this was one of the best books I've read all year! You must get it! I think it's one of Lacy Williams's best books ever!"

—LANA, GOODREADS

"Beautiful, sweet romance that raises hope in God and second chances He gives. What a first book in the series! Add to this a Robin Hood vibe, broken but eager to love and be loved characters, a small town with all that's good and all that's bad, and you'll give yourself a gift by reading this novel."

—NATASHA, GOODREADS

"This is a very touching tale of a woman who is a dedicated schoolteacher, in her own hometown. You will enjoy every moment as Lacy presents a moving and challenging story."

—JUDY, GOODREADS

"Fun and heartfelt mail-order bride romance. Loved it. Charming characters."

—MARIANNE, GOODREADS

"I really enjoyed Merritt and Jack's story of love and redemption. There's a hint of faith weaved into the story which I love."

—NIDA, GOODREADS

"I was hooked right from the start! Jack is mysterious and closed off, but as his story unfolds, you begin to see his huge desire to right injustices, his kind but broken heart, his sense of worthlessness, his longing to be loved and wanted. I enjoyed the story very much and am excited to see to where this series will take me."

—APRIL, GOODREADS

"I really enjoyed reading this book! It's romance with a bit of intrigue! I was hooked from the very beginning! I enjoy Lacy Williams' books very much! I look forward to the next one!"

—JEANETTE, GOODREADS

A
CONVENIENT
Heart

WIND RIVER MAIL-ORDER BRIDES

A CONVENIENT *Heart*

LACY WILLIAMS

sunrise PUBLISHING

A Convenient Heart
Wind River Mail-Order Brides, Book 1

Published by Sunrise Media Group LLC
Copyright © 2024 by Lacy Williams

ISBN: 978-1-963372-24-3

All Scripture quotations, unless otherwise indicated, are taken from the King James Version.

For more information about Lacy Williams, visit her website at lacywilliams.net.

Cover Design: Lacy Williams and Sarah Erredge

Wind River Mail-Order Brides

To my family.

A PERSON MAY THINK THEIR OWN WAYS ARE RIGHT,
BUT THE LORD WEIGHS THE HEART.

Proverbs 21:2

One

December 1892

M ISS HARDING, PAUL COPIED FROM
my slate!"
Merritt Harding stood beside a school desk
with one finger pointing at a line from *McGuffey's Eclectic
Reader* while little Clarissa Ewing struggled to sound out
a difficult word.

The tiny town of Calvin, Wyoming, had seen growth
over the past years, and her one-room school was bursting
at the seams with students.

"Miss Harding, he's copying my mannerisms again!"

With a prayer for patience slipping silently from her
lips, she patted Clarissa on the shoulder and left the girl
to sound out the words on the page.

Ignoring whispers from the front of the classroom, Merritt turned toward the back of the room, where the older
students were seated.

Thirteen-year-old Daniel Quinn had his arms crossed and was glaring at twelve-year-old Paul Gowen, who was indeed sitting in an identical pose, down to the pinch in his lips.

"Boys, what are we supposed to be working on?" she asked.

Both boys swung identical mulish looks at her. She didn't know whether to laugh or cry.

"He's mocking me!" Daniel cried.

Indeed, Paul mouthed the very same words.

Daniel was new to her classroom this year, his parents having moved to town last summer. She'd taught Paul in this schoolroom since he was six years old.

The two boys were alike in nearly every way. She'd been stumped since the first week of school, unable to understand how they had ended up as rivals instead of friends.

The whispers from the front of the room had grown in volume. A glance in that direction revealed Clarissa with her head bent over her book, lips moving as she silently read. Her seatmate was distracted by whatever conversation was happening amongst the six students in the three desks in front of her.

Merritt tapped the desk in front of Paul. "Why don't you continue your arithmetic work from my desk? Take your slate and chalk with you."

For a moment, she thought he would argue, but he reluctantly stood up and tucked his slate beneath his arm to trudge to her wooden desk at the front of the classroom. There were thick books stacked on one corner of the desk and paintbrushes lined up along the opposite side, but the center surface was clear. He should be able to do his work there.

"Please keep working," she told Daniel before she walked to the front of the room. With every step, the whispers became more muted until she stood before the front two desks with her eyebrows raised.

"Would you like to share with the rest of the class?" she asked Harriet Ferguson. The eight-year-old was small for her age and hadn't joined the schoolroom until last school year.

Harriet flushed and ducked her head, folding her hands in her lap as if Merritt had meted out a grand punishment, not asked a simple question.

"We was wonderin' if it's time to start practicin' for the pageant yet." Harriet's seatmate, five-year-old Samuel Ferguson, was practically bouncing on the wooden bench.

The slate-gray winter sky outside the window was no help determining the hour. It had been threatening snow all day, but only an occasional flake had danced past the window today.

Merritt consulted the watch pinned at her shoulder. "We've another half hour of work at least." She made her voice loud enough for the entire class to hear.

She felt the collective sigh of impatience and heard one audible groan. Though her glance encompassed the entire room, she couldn't tell where it had come from.

The Christmas pageant was scheduled to take place in this very classroom on Monday evening, a mere seven days from now.

Christmas was three days after that.

Between the two events, it was no wonder her students were restless and distracted. After nearly ten years in her position as Calvin's schoolteacher, Merritt expected it. Just like the tradition of holding the pageant in the schoolhouse had been upheld since she'd sat in one of the desks as a student, it was also tradition that the closer the performance loomed, the more distracted her students would be.

She had her own reasons for being distracted. This day had stretched interminably long already. *How* much longer until dismissal?

She'd be happy if she could wrangle fifteen more minutes of work out of her students. Then they could all practice reciting lines. A glance at the nearly completed canvas backdrop leaning against the wall at the back of the classroom made her shoulders droop slightly. She'd meant to make more progress on that project over the weekend but had spent her time planning meals for the next few days, shopping for each one as the special occasion it was, and scrubbing and dusting her entire house from floor to ceiling.

The work will get done, she told herself.

But not tonight. Tonight she had an engagement.

"Miss Harding, what's this?"

Paul held up a folded piece of paper. One crossed with cramped handwriting in even lines. One that she recognized.

Paul must've opened the drawer in her desk and found the letter.

"That's personal—"

"Are you getting married?"

Her words tumbled over his blurted question. It was too much to hope that no one else had heard.

She felt sixteen pairs of eyes swing in her direction as she hurried toward her desk.

"That's private," she snapped.

Paul's eyes widened as she came to stand beside where he sat in the hard-backed wooden chair.

She rarely used such a tone with the children.

But as she took the letter from his hand and slipped it into the pocket of her skirt, she felt blazing heat in her cheeks and realized she was breathing hard, as if she'd run up here instead of walked.

"You're gettin' married?" Harriet asked in the sudden empty silence.

"Course she ain't." Bobby Flannery piped up from across the room. "Miss Harding is a spinster and everyone knows it."

His seatmate must've elbowed his side, because Bobby yelped. "What? My ma even said so."

"That ain't nice," Clarissa said. "Miss Harding is pretty enough to get her a man if she wanted one."

"Children—"

Merritt's attempt at regaining control of the class went unheeded. Two students began arguing about her looks while Paul said, "I thought you couldn't be our teacher anymore if you get married."

Little Samuel looked at her with sad eyes and a now-trembling lower lip. "You don't want to be our teacher no more?"

"Of course I do," she told him.

But it was more complicated than that.

"She's old!" A voice burst out from the middle of the room.

And Merritt felt her temper spark.

"Enough!" She rapped the edge of her desk with her ruler, and the children went silent.

Twenty-five might be a spinster here in the West—most girls married before they were eighteen—but Merritt wasn't *old*.

She bit back the words to defend herself, knowing that debating a ten-year-old would not be an effective use of her time. Though it was tempting.

"I was not planning to tell you this yet"—her heart pounded as she made her voice loud and clear—"but I am . . . possibly . . . considering getting married."

"To who?" demanded a single voice from the back before Merritt's raised eyebrow quelled any more noise.

"*If* you complete today's work diligently and make it through our rehearsal, I will tell you a bit more."

It had been years since she'd lost control of her classroom like this. Even longer since she'd had to resort to bribery. But these were desperate times.

Her plea worked, and the last hour of the day flew past—probably because she dreaded what the children would ask.

The inquisition was as terrible as she'd imagined, but she was able to shorten it a bit as she rushed the children into their coats and out the door.

"I have known him for months." Technically true, though she'd never met her intended groom in person.

"He is a businessman." John had told her about investing in the railroad, though she hadn't understood it all from his letters. There would be time to discuss it at length soon enough.

"No, he isn't from around here." They hadn't discussed where they would live, other than agreeing that she needed to stay and finish the school term as her contract stipulated.

"Where did we meet? I answered an ad in a newspaper." These last words were said as she ushered the children out the door with her own woolen cape on and arms wide lest they dawdle any longer.

As she crossed out of the doorway, she caught sight of a familiar figure standing on the boardwalk just outside.

Drew McGraw. Her cousin and his three younger brothers owned a ranch well outside of town. She hadn't seen him in weeks, and he had a couple of days' worth of scruff on his jaw.

Her stomach was already twisty with anticipation and nerves as she crossed the boardwalk to him, watching the last of her students scurry toward their homes.

"What's this I just overheard?" He stretched out his arms as she walked toward him.

"What are you doing in town?" She asked the question as she joined in the affectionate hug. Maybe he'd be distracted . . .

But he was just as inquisitive as one of her students. He squeezed her shoulders, then stepped back to look into her face. "You met someone?"

She bit her lip and nodded. Icy wind bit at her cheeks but didn't cool the blush there.

"How come you haven't told the family?"

She saw the hint of hurt in his eyes and felt a pang of remorse. "I wanted to make certain that it . . . that he . . . "

She couldn't say the words aloud. There was still a part of her that worried that John would step off the train, take one look at her, and change his mind about the whole thing. Finding a husband to marry, bearing children of her own . . . her long-held dreams were coming true. Finally.

Drew didn't seem to know what to say to that, and that was all right too.

"Did you bring the children with you?" she asked.

Drew's thirteen-year-old son David, ten-year-old daughter Josephine, and five-year-old daughter Tillie were as close as if they were Merritt's own nieces and nephew, and Merritt missed them dearly.

"Not this time. Gotta grab a load of supplies and head back. Wanted to check if you're still coming for Christmas."

In the excitement of John's arrival, she'd forgotten about her promise to come and stay with the McGraw cousins for Christmas next week.

She'd be a married woman by then.

And John already knew how much her cousins meant to her. "I'll be there."

We'll be there.

The train whistle blew, the sound carried on a stiff wind, still far in the distance.

Her gaze flicked toward the end of town where the station was located. Her heart pounded.

"I've got to go," she said. "I'm meeting . . . him."

This was the moment her life would change forever.

"We're supposed to get married on Sunday. That's less than a week away. I mean, isn't it a lark? When I get off the train, she'll be looking for my hat and coat." He patted a red flower—a poppy?—in his lapel pocket.

Jack Easton didn't turn his head from where he sat in the railroad car. He didn't have to. Between the quiet, mostly empty compartment, a reflection in the glass window beside him, and the acoustics in the arch of the train car, the young man's conversation with an older gentleman who wore a neatly trimmed gray beard, in the seat across from him, carried perfectly to Jack's ear.

"She's a schoolteacher, been in the classroom for years," the young man went on.

"How many years?" Gray Beard asked.

Both men were dressed in suits—not the best quality, but a sign they were doing all right financially.

"Nine, I think." The younger man wore a bowler hat that made him look a mite foolish.

Jack favored a cowboy hat, but he'd lost his in a barroom scuffle a few days ago and hadn't replaced it yet. He riffled one hand through his hair at the empty feeling on his head.

"Nine years in the classroom?" Gray Beard sounded skeptical. Jack couldn't see his face in the reflection, but he had a clear view of the prospective groom's face. "Don't you think she's a little . . . long in the tooth?"

It was a rude thing to say, and Jack took offense on the unknown bride's behalf.

"She's twenty-five." But the groom suddenly looked uncertain.

"Or that's what she wants you to think. She could be lying. She might be forty."

It seemed to Jack that a schoolteacher would probably be someone upstanding in the community. Why would she lie? Especially when a lie about her age would be instantly revealed when the two met.

"What's wrong with her, anyway? Why'd she need to get a husband from a mail-order ad?"

The groom obviously hadn't considered anything like this, and Jack watched in the reflection as the man tugged at his shirt collar and then swallowed hard. "I've jumped into this, haven't I? Maybe I should've thought about it longer than I did."

Jack lost track of the conversation as he watched the landscape change outside the window. The woods and trees they'd been passing through opened up to a plain where everything was dusted with snow. The Laramie Mountains were visible in the far distance, purple shadows against the gray sky.

"Next stop, Calvin, Wyoming!" The conductor's voice called out, and then the man himself passed through the train car.

Jack had been all over the West in the past few years. Montana, Nevada, Colorado. He'd never stopped in Calvin. Passed through once and judged it too small.

But that'd been . . . three years ago? Maybe things had changed.

"Perhaps I should go home." The groom's voice sounded clear as a bell, and Jack saw that he'd loosened his tie now.

He took off his bowler hat and ran his hand through his hair, clearly agitated.

He'd be an easy mark across the poker table. His tells were as big as a brand on a cow's hindquarters.

"You don't want to meet her? What if she's a great beauty?" Gray Beard said. Was the man toying with the groom? He seemed to be playing devil's advocate now.

"It's almost Christmas," the young groom said.

Christmas.

Jack should find a game. Put aside a few dollars and hole up in a hotel room. Shops would be closed during the holiday. Restaurants too.

Jack didn't have a home to go back to. No one to celebrate with.

And he liked it that way. The nomadic life he lived suited him just fine.

He decided to stretch his legs. Standing up, he slipped his leather satchel over his head and shoulder. He had to hold on to the seat in front of him with one hand as the train swayed and rocked.

Jack strode through the nearly empty train car, then moved through the door at the end and into the next car over.

This one had a small water closet, its door slightly ajar, and was more crowded, with people in almost every seat. Many had packages around their feet or on their laps. Another sign of Christmas.

The conductor was calling out, and several people stood up in this train car, moving toward the door.

The brakes weren't screeching yet, but Jack could feel the slowing motion.

Looking down the car, he recognized the head of dark hair beneath a ten-gallon hat, the matching dark-brown mustache. The man was a head taller than most other travelers in the train car, and his lined face showed hard living.

Morris.

Jack turned to go back the way he'd come. He didn't have any desire to bump into Morris.

But two passengers blocked his way back into the other train car, and the only exit was to slip into the water closet.

Jack latched the door behind him.

He had a revolver at his hip, though he'd only had occasion to use it shooting cans off a branch or fence post. It was mostly for show, to keep other poker players from trying to rob him.

But Morris was a hired gun for the owner of a silver mine back in Colorado. Jack had judged him as unpredictable the last time he'd seen him.

The conductor called out again, his voice sounding just outside the water closet door. He must be returning through the compartment and re-entering the car Jack had left.

"I'm looking for a man named Jack Easton."

That was Morris's voice. He must've followed the conductor. Sounded like he was standing right outside the water closet.

"He's got some aliases," Morris went on.

Whatever the conductor said in response, it was muffled.

"He's got light hair. Wears a beard sometimes. Ugly as sin."

There was a tiny spotted looking glass high on one wall, and Jack glanced in it now. His nose had been broken once, a long time ago. It had the slightest bend in it. His eyes had crow's feet from being in the sun.

He wasn't ugly.

At least, not judging by the looks he got from the women who kept company in the saloons. He never took them up on the offers their eyes made.

Jack appeared a little disreputable, maybe, with the scruff on his chin—hadn't seen a barber in weeks. Not ugly.

"He stole five hundred bucks from a friend of mine. I'd like to get it back."

Jack watched in the looking glass as his reflection scowled.

He hadn't stolen a thing from Clark Henshaw. Jack had won at the poker table fair and square—without even a card up his sleeve.

He'd learned early on how cards made more sense than people. How to predict what was coming up next—ace or deuce or anything in between.

Reading people had come later, out of necessity. He'd learned to predict when a fist might come his way and that an empty bottle meant trouble.

He was good at reading people now. And he didn't drink much. Saw it as a weakness after what he'd been through as a child. Which meant that the longer the night went on at a poker table and the more drunk the men around him got, the sharper Jack's senses became.

He didn't have to cheat to win.

And the men he played could afford to lose. He didn't play otherwise.

"I'd like to get the money back to my friend," Morris said.

Good luck.

Jack had fifty cents in his pocket. He'd passed the winnings from Henshaw's table to a group of widows whose husbands had died in a mine accident. Henshaw had sent men into an unsafe shaft, and they'd been lost to a cave-in. The unscrupulous owner had made no reparations to the widows left behind—women who had children to feed but no source of income. Likely those women had paid overdue bank notes or settled up accounts at the local general store.

Jack had righted that wrong.

There was no money for Morris to collect.

And Jack didn't want to think about how the man might try to enforce the debt. He winced.

The train braked with a hiss and screech. The voices outside the water closet rose and fell as passengers disembarked.

Jack edged open the door to find the small vestibule empty.

He cautiously moved out of the water closet and tried to guess where Morris had gone. Would he get off the train at this stop?

Jack crept through the doors and back onto his original train car.

It was empty.

As he tried to guess whether Morris had gone through here, Jack rushed forward to see that both the young groom and Gray Beard were gone.

But the groom's coat and hat were abandoned on the seat. The coat was crumpled, flower hanging precariously.

The door opened at the end of the train car, and Jack's pulse pounded as if he'd drawn a pair of aces.

It wasn't Morris but a grandmotherly-looking woman. Short.

Over her head, Jack had a clear view of Morris's back, his head and shoulders, in the train car beyond.

And then Morris started to turn.

Jack ducked, instinct pushing him to don the abandoned coat. He quickly shoved his arms into the sleeves, hastily pulling the coat over his own. His satchel hung awkwardly between the coats, but he ignored it for now. He reached for the hat, mashing it low on his head. It wasn't much of a disguise, but maybe if he moved quickly, Jack would be all right.

He kept his back to where Morris had been and walked calmly away.

"All aboard!" the conductor called from the platform outside.

He couldn't stay on this train with Morris on board.

He stepped off the train and onto the platform. Another train would pass by. Maybe this afternoon or maybe tomorrow. He'd get on it and find a place to hole up for Christmas.

"John?" A feminine voice called out.

He turned on instinct and came face-to-face with a woman who was pretty as a picture.

Snow dusted her dark hair, pulled behind her head in a low bun. Her dark eyes were intelligent, and he saw a moment of hesitation pass through them before she took one step closer, her pert chin rising just slightly.

"It's me." She sounded the way he felt—breathless. Anticipation shimmered between them.

"I'm . . . I'm your bride."

Two

J ACK DOFFED THE HAT, AWARE THAT Morris might be looking out the train window. But his focus had shifted from the man somewhere behind him to the beautiful woman in front of him.

This was the long-in-the-tooth spinster that the young groom had been worried about meeting?

Her groom was a fool.

He glanced around quickly—maybe it wasn't too late for the young man. Jack could give back his hat and coat, explain the mix-up . . .

But the young man was nowhere to be seen. Was he hiding on the train somewhere?

The platform was filled with travelers, some pushing through the crowd to rush onto the train. Brakes hissed as they released.

Someone passed behind the schoolteacher, bumping into her in the same moment that the train whistle blasted.

Off-kilter, she started to stumble and extended one hand—at the same moment that Jack reached out to steady her.

She was wearing gloves, while he was bare-handed.

And yet he still felt a beat of shock at the moment their hands connected and clasped—like the roar of dynamite biting into the mountain near those mines in Colorado.

Her eyes searched his face, as if she'd felt it too.

He dropped her hand and the moment ended. He flexed his hand and felt a phantom echo of that hand clasp.

A gust of wind blustered through and pushed her skirts against her legs. She touched the back of her hair as if making sure her pins were still in place.

It was cold out here.

And high time he went about making his escape. He glanced back toward the train as it chugged once and then twice more.

"You must be hungry after such a long journey. I've reserved a table for us at the hotel dining room."

It wasn't a question.

"And Mrs. Stoll has your room ready at the boarding-house. I checked with her this morning."

She glanced around him, her brow furrowing suddenly. "Where's . . . do you have a trunk?"

The missing groom probably did, but all Jack carried was his satchel. He patted it now. "I've got all I need right here."

A shadow passed through her eyes, followed by the tiniest squint.

"Hey, you!"

A shout from the train turned Jack's head, though he tried to be discreet.

Morris was there, standing in the open doorway of the train, which was pulling out of the station.

He wasn't looking Jack's way, though. His glare was aimed at someone talking to one of the porters, across the platform.

But then he turned his scowl in Jack's direction. "John. John?"

As Jack turned back to the woman before him, heart thrumming in his ears, he realized she'd said his name—or what she thought was his name. John was the groom?

He needed to get off the platform before Morris caught sight of him and jumped off the slow-moving train.

He slipped his hand beneath the teacher's elbow and nudged her toward the stairs he could see not far away, effectively turning both their backs to Morris.

"Jack." He corrected her before he'd thought better of it. "Call me Jack."

Her eyes searched his face. There was a tiny pinch at the top of her nose between her brows, and for one wild moment, he imagined pressing a kiss there.

What had come over him?

Two minutes of pretending to be some lovesick groom and he was imagining a closeness with this woman—this stranger—that didn't exist.

Maybe he'd fallen asleep on the train and this was simply a strange dream.

He didn't even know her name.

He realized it as their boots hit the wooden boardwalk

at the base of the stairs. Like everything else, it was dusted with snow.

"The hotel is serving roasted chicken tonight. I know that's one of your favorites."

She was nervous, though she hadn't shrugged away from his touch.

She'd put on a good show on the train platform, with that raised chin and confidence behind her statements, the plans she'd made.

But experience had taught him to see past her bluff, and he could feel the slight tremor that ran through her when she glanced at him as they walked.

And he wasn't a cruel man. The words to tell her the truth, that there'd been a mistake, were right there on the tip of his tongue.

"Evening, miss!" A man sweeping the boardwalk planks in front of the grocery stopped to wave at them.

Moments later, a boy of fifteen or so, toting boxes down the boardwalk, actually stopped to tip his hat. "You finished your Christmas shopping?" he asked the schoolmarm.

"All done. How about you?" she answered sweetly.

And in the big glass window of a dress shop, the woman arranging a lace shawl over the shoulders of a mannequin stopped her work to wave.

Did the schoolmarm know every single person in town? She must.

The sense of community in the interactions, in the warm smile she had for everyone, made Jack uncomfortable. It was so . . . cloying.

He never stayed anywhere long enough to put down roots. And he liked it that way.

As they passed by a saloon, two men stomped out of the swinging doors. They were arguing loudly, and even from here Jack could smell the whiskey.

The schoolmarm's nose wrinkled. "You'll have to excuse that. It's a disgrace to have four saloons in one small town."

"You don't think a couple of cowpokes like those deserve to let loose on their night off?"

She blinked at him, her brow wrinkling. She gave a slight head shake and said, "I'm not one to judge, but I am friends with the local marshal. The instances of unruly behavior and public drunkenness have become overwhelming. The saloons should take their business elsewhere."

I'm friends with the marshal. If there were any words she could've said to doom an instant camaraderie, those worked.

Her highfalutin vocabulary was like drawing an offsuit when one almost had a flush. Maybe the young groom had been right to abscond. If Jack could have been sure Morris had stayed on that train, he might've slipped away this very moment.

But the truth of his identity, the words to excuse himself, stayed locked behind his teeth as they walked down the sleepy main street. His stomach grumbled. He'd sit through supper, then tell her the truth and get outta here.

The town was still as small as he remembered, though there was another saloon around the corner from the bank, piano music and light spilling out into the quiet street.

The hotel was warm inside, and he surrendered his

coats—both of them—to the front desk attendant. The lobby was decked out with red ribbons and bows and even a swag of pine across the wide front desk.

Seated at the cloth-covered table, the schoolmarm was even prettier in the lamplight. It gilded the edges of her eyelashes gold.

I'm friends with the marshal. The reminder echoed inside him.

She was also prim, folding her hands in her lap when he would've slouched in his seat.

"I'll walk you to the boardinghouse after supper. We'll meet with the preacher tomorrow evening. There are a few things he wants to go over. I know he wants to meet with you privately a time or two before the wedding."

She barely drew a breath before going on. "Since my students will be on Christmas break, we'll have several days to settle into the house before I have to go back into the classroom." A blush pinked her cheeks. "My teaching contract expires in May, and the school board won't hire me back once we are married. Of course, you already know all this . . . "

Her nervous rambling stopped, and she finally looked up at him and he winked. "Why don't we make it through supper before we plan the rest of our lives?"

Her brows pinched again as the waiter, a young man in a starched shirt and dark trousers, brought two mugs of steaming coffee.

His companion thanked the man in a quiet murmur. He caught her distracted glance to the side and turned his head to see what she was looking at.

Two little girls sat on their knees at a nearby table as they peered above the chair backs to watch the schoolmarm. A man and woman—their parents?—were eating and conversing, not paying attention.

"I trust your journey was favorable."

He blinked and brought his gaze back to the schoolmarm, who seemed determined to ignore the other table.

He shrugged.

She frowned, just a little. "Will you miss being at home for Christmas?"

The innocent question hit a soft spot in his underbelly. "There's nothing for me there." His words sounded sharp, a perfect pairing with the way he felt inside.

He'd thought he could playact his way through supper, but this was more than he'd bargained for.

A giggle from nearby drew his eyes, and now the two little girls were even more obvious in their wide-eyed stares. Their parents still hadn't noticed that they were almost falling out of their seats to watch Jack and his companion.

"Friends of yours?" he asked, raising one eyebrow.

She was clearly torn between smiling and frowning.

"Two of my students." She settled for a pinched smile. "As I mentioned in my letters, there's not much privacy for a schoolmarm in such a small town." She grimaced slightly and played with the napkin in her lap. "I'm afraid my students discovered one of your letters just this afternoon and . . . well, they were distracted for the rest of the school day."

He tipped his head toward the table with the girls. "You want to invite them over to say hello?"

He didn't wait for her answer, heard her soft noise of protest when he turned in his seat and waved the two girls over.

Their eyes grew big in their faces, and they glanced at each other before scampering over.

"Hello, Miss Harding!" two girlish voices chorused.

Miss Harding. He had a surname.

"Hello. I'm Jack—" He covered for the way he'd cut off his sentence by extending his hand for them to shake. He'd almost introduced himself with his real name.

The first little girl, two inches taller than her sister, shook his hand while looking gravely serious.

Miss Harding sighed quietly. "This is Ellie and Lillian Kilman. Two of my best students."

The younger girl, who was pumping his hand up and down, was beaming at him. "She says that about all of us. Are you Miss Harding's new husband?"

"Not yet."

A glance across the table revealed Miss Harding's cheeks stained with a rosy blush.

"Mr. Crosby has only just stepped off the train," she told the girls.

"It sure is nice to meet two of the prettiest young ladies in town. Almost as pretty as your Miss Harding."

The woman was looking past the girls to wave at their parents, but at his words, her gaze snapped back to him.

If anything, her blush grew more pronounced.

Some boyish urge inside him wanted to see it again.

Ellie and Lillian giggled.

"We've been practicing for our Christmas pageant," Ellie said. "You're going to come to watch, aren't you?"

"Everyone in town will be there," said her younger sister.

Miss Harding was the first to speak. "I'm sure Mr. Crosby has seen his share of pageants and played his part when he was your age."

She'd be wrong about that.

For a moment, he was kicked back to his childhood—a time he didn't like to think about. Going to bed hungry at night. Chores all day—backbreaking work. Never knowing when he was going to get switched for something he'd done wrong—or something *she* imagined he'd done.

His guardians hadn't believed in schooling, not for him. After he'd left the orphanage at eleven, he hadn't seen the inside of a school building.

"We'll see," he said.

He wouldn't be in Calvin when the pageant rolled around. But he hadn't said an outright lie either.

Miss Harding was watching him, and for once, all his skill at reading people failed him. He couldn't tell what she was thinking, but that little furrow above her nose was back.

Merritt placed her fork across her half-full plate and folded her hands in her lap.

The nerves she'd felt since the first moment she'd come face-to-face with John—Jack—hadn't dissipated one bit.

Food gone, he sipped his coffee across the table. The waiter had already taken his plate.

He ate like a man who worked long hours of physical

labor, like her cousins. Or like a man who'd grown up not knowing when he'd eat his next meal.

It didn't fit with what she knew of John through his letters.

Everything about the man was incongruous with what she'd imagined.

He was quiet. Not once while they'd eaten had he rushed in to fill a silence. He watched the people around them.

But she'd also felt the intensity of his attention. Never once while she'd chattered had he looked bored or uninterested.

As pretty as your Miss Harding.

She hadn't expected the compliment.

Or how his very presence, sitting across the table, seemed larger than life somehow. As if he wasn't quite real.

He was *too* handsome. Maybe that was the reason her stomach was knotted.

His eyes changed color in the low lamplight. Sometimes blue. Sometimes hazel or green.

She'd expected him clean-shaven, but the stubble at his jaw somehow made him seem more rugged. The slightest crook in his nose should've ruined the visage but somehow only enhanced it.

This was all wrong.

The beat of her pulse, which hadn't steadied all evening. The flutter of her heart when he turned his gaze on her.

This was supposed to be a *transaction*. A signature on a piece of paper, an amiable, friendly affection. She'd hoped for a simple, pleasant sense of camaraderie. Someone to provide companionship on lonely prairie winter nights that stretched long.

But what she felt for John—Jack—this instant attraction . . . it felt dangerous.

She scooped up her coffee cup and held it with both hands in front of her, a sort of protective measure.

"You told me about your business deal in your last letter," she said. "Were you able to complete it satisfactorily?"

A shadow chased through Jack's eyes. He set his coffee mug on the table and smiled that dangerous smile at her. "We'll have plenty of time to talk about all that later."

There was something about the slight hesitation behind his words that unsettled her.

Or maybe it was the man himself.

Suddenly, thinking through all her carefully laid plans made her feel the slightest bit claustrophobic. Should she delay the wedding?

Was she having second thoughts? Or simply nervous that the time had finally come?

She shored up her smile. "That's right. After we're married Sunday morning, I'll have the pageant on Monday evening, but school will be out of session for a week. We'll have a lot of time to get to know each other after that."

She'd thought they'd gotten to know each other through the letters they'd exchanged.

But the virile man in front of her was nothing like the dry, fact-filled letters she'd received.

"Look, I need to tell you—" He glanced around. The dining room had emptied some as the evening had worn on, other diners wanting to get home to their warm houses or go to bed. But there were still several couples and a businessman or two sitting nearby. "Do you want to take a walk?"

Take a walk? She'd imagined sitting in the warm dining room for hours, getting to know each other. She had so many questions about his family, his business, his thoughts. Was he already bored?

"We can walk to the boardinghouse," she said, infusing her words with a smile she didn't feel.

"I don't—"

But Jack's words were cut off when a shout came from outside. A shadow passed by the window overlooking the street, and then someone burst through the front doors of the hotel lobby.

"Fire!"

The shout was enough to send her heart racing.

Jack jumped up from the table as quickly as she did, and they raced into the lobby. He had the presence of mind to grab his coats and her cape, and as they dashed outside into the icy wind, she was grateful to put her arms through the sleeves and button it up.

"Where?" she asked as she bumped into a man—Will from the livery, rushing down the boardwalk.

Will's grim expression brought on a shock of terror. "The school, I think."

No!

She glanced at Jack. "You don't have to—but I must go."

She didn't even know what she meant to say, only knew that she had to reach the school, had to help.

She was dimly aware of him pressing close behind her as

she made her way through the crowd toward the school. It was only a block away, around two corners, but time had slowed somehow and she couldn't breathe . . .

Everyone in town seemed to have come out. At least, that's what the press of bodies felt like.

She saw the flicker of orange against the cloudy sky before she was close enough to see the building.

Smoke burned her nose and brought tears to her eyes.

She pushed as close as she could, joined a bucket brigade, and passed bucket after bucket of water with icy fingers. Time seemed to crawl, but she also felt the pressing urgency. Could they save the school? More buckets passed, each one growing heavier and heavier as her arms tired. She bumped shoulders with the man at her side—the doctor, she realized belatedly.

Keep going.

Ash rained down on her bare head, swirling amongst the snowflakes on the breeze as her mind pinwheeled. Her hands were numb from the cold. Her thoughts whirled.

Had she closed the stove's ash pit after she'd set things in order for tomorrow morning?

Had she doused the two lamps they used when cloudy winter weather blotted out the natural light from the windows?

There was a tin pail full of kindling and twigs near the stove. Had a spark somehow jumped out of the stove when she'd been closing things down?

She would've sworn she'd completed her routine as usual, but in the chaos of her own excitement and the children's finding out about Jack . . . had she missed something?

Was this her fault?

The flames licked higher. She was stationed next to the restaurant, two dozen yards away from the school building, yet she still felt the frightening heat from the fire.

Was there any way the building could be saved?

"Stop for a minute."

A man's voice interrupted her frantic movements as she tried to pass the next bucket along.

"Miss Harding. Stop."

But she couldn't—

And then two strong hands wrapped around her upper arms, and she was bodily moved out of the bucket-brigade line.

"Miss Harding!"

She fought against the hands holding her, moving her away from the chaos of those fighting the fire.

It was Jack, she realized through her overwhelming emotion.

"Stop! Miss Harding!"

She shoved against his chest as they stopped several yards away from the bucket brigade, on the boardwalk across the street. "Why don't you call me Merritt?" she demanded. Her chest heaved on the words.

She hadn't realized she was crying until he pressed a handkerchief in her hands.

"Merritt." Her name was spoken in a tender drawl.

The moment she stopped fighting, her energy flagged. Her knees gave way but she didn't fall. Because Jack pulled her in close against his chest.

His coat was open, she realized, as the warmth of his

body slowly seeped into her skin. The small heat bit her skin, almost frozen from the air outside and drenched with water.

"You'll catch your death," he chided her, one hand running up and down her back.

When had she let her cheek press against his broad chest?

She couldn't seem to summon the wherewithal to straighten, to move away from him.

He brushed at her cheek with one hand, fingers cold, as more tears ran silently down her cheeks.

"My school," she said with a sob.

His jaw pressed into the top of her head. "I'm sorry. I'm sorry."

The skin on her hands and wrists pricked and burned where she was tucked beneath his coat, feeling returning painfully to what had been numb extremities. How long had they been out in the elements?

"Over an hour," Jack murmured into her hair.

Had she said the words aloud?

An hour that the school building had been burning. There was no saving it.

"No," he said, and she must've been speaking her thoughts aloud again. "The wind picked up, and the men are trying to keep the fire from spreading."

Oh.

She thought of all the books and papers, lost. The slates, the chalkboard.

"The pageant backdrops," she mumbled.

"Hmm?"

"The children will be devastated. They've worked hard to get ready for the pageant."

And what would they do without a classroom when school was meant to resume?

Her thoughts tumbled like one of the snowflakes tossed about on the wind.

"They could still perform the pageant without the back-drops, couldn't they?"

It wouldn't be the same.

But she appreciated his attempt at comforting her.

She pushed back from his embrace, brushing at the hair that had fallen from its pins. Cold slithered at the neck of her cape.

She was a mess. No doubt her face was streaked with soot and she was a soggy mess.

But Jack was looking at her in the flickering light in a way she couldn't understand.

She swayed nearer and he frowned. "You've got soot . . . " His voice trailed off as his thumb brushed her jaw.

And then he was the one who took a step back, leaving her off-balance and wobbly.

Someone called out, and she became aware of several men at the corner of the boardwalk. Was that why Jack had stepped away from her? He must've been more aware of their surroundings than she had been in her upset. Had Jack been protecting her reputation? Keeping the men from seeing the private moment between the two of them?

She watched his profile as his eyes tracked the men.

Jack was a surprise in every way.

But as her gaze took in the last of the dying flames and

the skeleton of what had once been her beloved classroom, she was glad for his presence. Glad that she wasn't standing on the boardwalk alone with this awful hopelessness swamping her.

How was she supposed to finish out the school year without a classroom?

Three

W E'LL REBUILD. THE CHILDREN NEED a school."

"Where's the money gonna come from? Town's got no budget for rebuilding."

The conversation between the two male voices washed over Jack, though he was hardly paying attention.

He was having some trouble looking away from Merritt. She'd given him her name in a storm of tears hours ago, and he had felt such a punch of connection.

Early morning sunlight was spilling over the horizon. Sometime in the wee hours, the clouds and snow had moved off. It looked like it would be a cold, sunny day later. Right now, everyone who had gathered on the streets was covered in gray soot. Wisps of smoke and steam filtered up into the sky from the ashes and coals that had once been the school building.

Merritt was covered in soot too. She had a smudge of it right on her nose, and he wanted to do something about it—but he didn't dare.

For one, she was surrounded by other people.

But the real reason he was poking through the ashes with a long-handled spade, as far away from her as he could manage, was because it was time for him to go.

Past time.

He'd gotten too involved already.

This wasn't his home, and she wasn't for him.

His body ached from weariness. No one out here had slept, and hauling all that water had taxed his muscles. In a moment, he was going to slip away into one of the nearby alleyways and disappear.

Something about the thought was like the last draw in a poker hand revealing a worthless card.

"So, you're Miss Harding's beau?"

A youthful voice cracked on the words and Jack looked up.

Two boys of roughly twelve or thirteen had approached, both holding hoes.

"I'm Jack," he said instead of answering the question.

He stuck the spade upright into the ground and held it with his left hand while he extended his right.

The two boys ignored his outstretched hand in favor of digging into the rubble with their hoes. They were enthusiastic with their efforts, and ash flew up into the air.

Jack moved a step away from them and tried not to cough. His lungs still felt a little singed.

"I'm Daniel," grunted the nearer boy.

"And I'm Paul," said the other, who was maybe an inch taller.

"I suppose you two are former students of Miss Harding?"

His assumption that they were older puffed out their chests. The two boys glanced at each other.

"Naw, we're in our last year now," Daniel said as he poked at the charred rubble.

Jack nudged a large piece of still-smoking wood with his spade. "Do you have plans after your schooling?"

"My pa works at the bank," Daniel said. "He thinks maybe I can go to college if I study hard enough."

Paul was turned away from Daniel, and the other boy didn't see the way he mimicked the last of his words. Was this opportunity a sore spot between the two?

"What about you?" Jack asked Paul.

The kid shrugged. "I dunno." He sent a resentful glare at Daniel, but the other boy didn't see it. "Miss Harding says I could be a doctor, but that's a lot more schooling."

And money.

Daniel scoffed. "Your pa is a farmer. How you gonna pay for doctor school?"

Paul dug his hoe into the ash and flipped it in Daniel's direction, sending a puff of ash wafting toward him.

"Hey!"

Jack cleared his throat, and the two boys frowned but settled down.

"What's Miss Harding like? As a teacher?" he asked.

"She's all right," Paul muttered, shoving his next scoop with a little more force than necessary.

"She's the best," Daniel said. "She's real good at explainin' complicated 'rithmetic problems, and she's patient when she's teaching the little kids to read."

"She's a good reader," Paul added. "She does different voices for different characters in the book."

"She even wrote the script for our Christmas pageant... " Daniel's voice trailed off as he surveyed the mess of what had been their school building.

It must have just hit him that the pageant wouldn't go on as they'd planned.

"It'll be all right," Jack said. "Your Miss Harding will figure something out."

He'd seen it himself. She was smart as a whip. And from what the boys had described, she was well liked in the classroom.

Paul leaned on his shovel, chin jutted out. "Anyways, we came over here to find out about you. Whadda you do for work?"

"A little of this, a little of that."

Daniel squinted at him. "What's that mean?"

The kid was smart too. Or had learned from his teacher. He hadn't accepted Jack's offhand answer.

"I travel to different places," Jack said. "And sometimes I find problems. And I fix them."

The kid seemed to think on that for a minute.

It was Paul who threw out the next question. "How come you needed a mail-order wife anyway?"

For a tick, as Paul tilted his head just so, Jack was thrown back in time—fifteen years, to when Dewey had worn the same narrow-eyed expression. And then Dewey's expression had changed as he'd smiled. His eyes had danced.

Are we going fishing tomorrow?

Jack heard the voice from his past as clearly as he did the two boys who were arguing right next to him.

Dewey had been a blood brother only in the sense that they had sworn it to each other after they had nicked their palms with a knife and pressed them together on a muggy summer morning.

Dewey had been three years younger than Jack and, while he might have had an occasional bout of orneriness, had been one of the kindest souls Jack had ever known.

Jack hadn't thought about him in a long time. It was too painful to recall the memories. And it was only a fluke that he had caught the faint resemblance of Paul to Dewey.

"Can't have you catching cold." The gruff female voice came only a moment before a woolen blanket was slipped over Jack's shoulders.

He blinked away the painful memories and caught sight of an older woman in a drab green dress with at least two more folded blankets in her arms. She was looking at the boys. "You lads need warming up?"

"No, ma'am," they chorused.

"That's what I thought. Mr. Jack has been out here all night, while you two've only been out for a bit."

Jack pointed to where Merritt was flanked by two women. "Merritt—Miss Harding has been out all night too."

"I'll go to her next." The matronly woman who'd delivered the blanket was watching Jack with dancing eyes.

"She sure did pick a good one. You jumped right in to help when we needed it."

He was opening his mouth to tell her that she was wrong—that Merritt hadn't picked him, that he didn't belong here—but the woman was already gone.

"That's Mrs. Stoll from the boardinghouse," Daniel murmured. "Yer lucky she likes you. She don't like hardly anybody."

That was the woman Jack would've stayed with if he'd been this John Crosby fellow?

Paul jerked his chin toward another woman, this one in her forties, with a coffee pot in one hand and tin mugs in the other. She was passing out a warm drink that would help the people still standing around.

"That's Mrs. Steele. She owns the café."

Jack had never seen anything like this. The townsfolk had stepped up to help, not just to stop the fire, but now they were rallying around each other. Figuring out how to fix things, keeping each other warm and fed.

It was like something out of a fairytale. He wasn't sure he believed in it. He sure knew that he didn't belong here.

The question was how best to slip away without causing any more trouble.

Merritt heard the husky laugh, and she couldn't help the way her head turned toward Jack.

He was poking through the debris at the edge of what had been the schoolhouse. Daniel and Paul stood nearby, both now leaning on their shovels while they talked to

Jack. Each boy watched him with rapt attention, and then Daniel said something as he waved his hands in an animated way.

Jack responded. She couldn't hear what he said, but it was clear that he had made an instant connection with the two boys.

Here was another unexpected side of Jack. She had thought that perhaps it would take a while for him to warm up to her students, or that he might only be casually interested in connecting with them socially.

For a moment, his gaze floated over the crowd, and then it crashed with hers. Her stomach pitched, and she raised one hand to wave at him.

He nodded, unsmiling.

She couldn't help but notice the distance between them. Ever since she had burst into tears in his arms hours ago, he'd been closed off. Had carefully avoided being close to her.

He'd put walls up.

It would be all right, she told herself. Everyone was exhausted after a sleepless night.

The crowd was dispersing slowly as families returned to their homes.

"I want a full investigation."

She glanced over her shoulder at the familiar voice and slightly hunched shoulders beneath a tailored coat. It was Mr. Polk, one of the school board members. He was a young father with a child not yet old enough for the classroom, but he had connections to prominent businessmen in town, including Billy Burns, who owned two of the saloons.

Polk's dark eyes cut to Merritt and then away. He was speaking to a woman in trousers, who had a badge pinned to the vest beneath her coat. Danna O'Grady was town marshal and one of Merritt's close friends.

"The school board will need to be informed immediately if there are any signs of willful negligence that caused the fire."

Merritt's shoulders tensed as her tired brain took a moment to process his words.

He thought Merritt had somehow caused the fire.

They had butted heads more than once over her teaching methods, her classroom discipline, and over this year's Christmas pageant. But for him to make such a terrible assumption . . .

She had half a mind to march up to him and set him straight. Only her own exhaustion and a check in her spirit—the echo of her thoughts from last night—kept her feet unmoving.

As tired as she was, her temper would have a short fuse. She didn't want to say something that couldn't be taken back. The man, along with two others, was responsible for overseeing her job.

"Don't let that blustering fool rile you up." The low voice from her side reminded Merritt that she wasn't alone. Mrs. Quinn, Daniel's mother, linked her arm with Merritt's so that their backs were to Danna and Mr. Polk.

"I closed up the school just the same as every other day," Merritt muttered to herself.

Mrs. Quinn patted her hand. "I know, dear. There's not an irresponsible bone in your body."

Mrs. Stoll was distributing blankets, and Merritt noticed that Jack had one around his shoulders. The woman offered one to Merritt, who declined with a shake of her head. She should go home. Try to sleep.

Looking at the empty lot, now littered with ashes and clumps of wood, just made her sad.

"It's a pity. But we'll rebuild," Mrs. Stoll said, following her gaze.

"Not soon enough," Merritt said. She had been worrying over the problem all night. They would need a place for lessons in the interim, before the building could be rebuilt. "And the children had worked so hard on the pageant . . ."

"There is no reason we couldn't hold the pageant at the church," Mrs. Quinn said.

"Or even the dance hall," Mrs. Stoll piped in.

She appreciated their enthusiasm to help find a solution, but the tradition in Calvin had long been to hold the pageant in the schoolhouse. There was no easy solution for the sadness that engulfed her. Even when a new schoolhouse was built, nothing would ever be the same. Of course, next Christmas she wouldn't be coordinating the pageant at all. In his letters, Jack had promised they would remain in Calvin until her teaching contract was up, but there had been no mention of whether he would want to live in her hometown permanently.

Merritt caught sight of Daniel and Paul racing off down the side street.

The boys were classroom rivals, but they'd put aside their differences to build one of the pageant backdrops.

All of the children, not just Paul and Daniel, would be devastated if the pageant didn't happen. It was a Christmas tradition. And for those two boys, it would be their last Christmas in her classroom.

Jack had stooped to talk to Harriet. Oh, and there was Samuel too. The five-year-old boy was sobbing inconsolably, while Harriet looked teary.

Merritt started toward them but stopped when she saw Jack speaking seriously to the boy. He slipped the blanket off his own shoulders and wrapped it around Samuel. It swamped his small body.

The boy sniffled and wiped one cheek with a corner of the blanket that covered his hand. He blinked, now calmer.

Jack had done that.

"I like your Jack," Mrs. Quinn said.

He wasn't hers yet.

Seeing him comfort Samuel made Merritt's breath catch. She'd dreamed of a family of her own for such a long time. She'd put aside those girlish dreams after her parents had moved back east. It had seemed more prudent to focus on her studies, but there had been times when she'd stared at the ceiling during lonely nights in a girls' dormitory at the normal college, and they'd slipped in when she couldn't bear the loneliness.

Her dreams had never abandoned her. They'd come back full force months ago, and Merritt had known she couldn't keep waiting for the right man to come along. She had to take action.

And here was Jack, settling his hat on top of Samuel's head.

Now Samuel was looking at her fiancé, blinking as he talked. Harriet looked happier too. Samuel even cracked a small smile.

Whatever Jack had said, he had calmed the boy down. He was good with kids.

It felt like a confirmation that Merritt had made the right choice.

"What does he do for work?" Mrs. Stoll asked absently.

Merritt knew she would be fielding questions until everyone in town knew the answers. "He's a businessman."

The older woman's brow wrinkled. "He is?" The skeptical tone to her voice made Merritt blink. "He doesn't seem like a businessman."

Before she could answer, the two women excused themselves.

"Miss Harding?" Henry, one of Merritt's former students, the young man who'd waited on them last night at the hotel, came alongside her. "Your beau forgot this last night."

He handed her Jack's leather satchel and was gone before she could say thank you.

She hadn't even realized Jack had forgotten it in their haste to fight the fire.

Jack's gaze narrowed on her, and he started making his way toward her.

Behind him, she saw that Samuel still wore his hat.

"Let me take that." His words were a command that

brooked no argument, and the way he was frowning made her hand it over quickly. He slipped it over his shoulders.

It shouldn't have bothered her that he'd wanted to take the satchel back, but something about the exchange niggled at her.

She tried to ignore it. Nodded to where he had just come from. "You left your hat."

He glanced quickly over his shoulder and back. Gone was the charming Jack from supper last night. "I never liked that hat. He can keep it."

She still felt the tension of walls up between them. Was Jack that discomforted that she'd wept in his arms? Other people still milled about, and suddenly, she was too tired to wonder or worry any more.

"I can walk you over to the boardinghouse," she said.

"Fine. Then we gotta talk."

Four

S HOULDN'T YOU BE AT HOME RESTING?"
At the familiar voice, Merritt turned from where
she'd been staring into space, standing in the center
of the empty dance hall. Danna strode inside, crossing the
echoing room to Merritt.

"I could ask you the same thing." Danna had been at
the site of the fire last night for just as long as Merritt had.
She had a two-month-old baby at home, along with her
toddler daughter.

This morning, after walking a silent Jack to the boardinghouse, Merritt had gone home to her tiny bungalow and
slept fitfully for a couple of hours. Turned out he hadn't
wanted to talk after all.

When she couldn't keep her eyes closed against the
winter sunlight seeping past the edges of her curtains any
longer, she'd dressed and come down here.

Merritt dropped her hands from her waist, slipping

the piece of paper and pencil into her skirt pocket. She'd thought to make a list of everything she would need for a makeshift classroom.

But the list was so long that she'd frozen, unable to write a thing. Her paper was blank.

"Are you all right?" Danna asked as she came to stand next to Merritt.

Merritt smiled. "Of course not." Danna knew how Merritt thrived on order. On knowing what today's plan would be, and tomorrow's . . .

Right now, she didn't know what the future held for her classroom.

Perhaps their friendship was unconventional. Danna was a woman in a man's job. Town marshal. She'd been a deputy for years before her first husband had passed away. She wore trousers and a vest beneath her slicker, a gun belt around her waist, and a silver star pinned to her chest.

Some around these parts thought she shouldn't have her job as marshal.

But she was good at it. And she still managed to be a good mother.

Merritt sighed. "Perhaps the church would be a better fit for a makeshift classroom. There are pews for the children to sit in."

The church building was right across the street from the burnt remains of the schoolhouse. She could only imagine the children's drooping shoulders as they arrived each day.

"We could put a few tables in here and they'd have a place to write. Have their books in front of them." Danna said the words with a calm assurance, motioning around the empty room. Merritt wished she felt the same confidence.

"We have no books or slates." She had a couple of teaching manuals at home that had been collecting dust on her personal bookshelf, but most of her teaching materials were gone as well.

"Chas and I are gonna put some readers on order with the general store. A donation, as it were."

Her heart swelled with gratitude toward her friend.

"That's very generous." She reached over to give Danna a hug. "Give Chas my thanks."

Startled to find her eyes pricking with tears, Merritt drew away and swiped at her cheeks with her fingertips.

She caught Danna's questioning gaze. "I'm exhausted, but I couldn't sleep." She explained the tears away.

"Hmm." Danna glanced around the cavernous space.

Merritt was already thinking about how some of her younger students would try to run and play in the large space.

"Let's go to the general store and borrow a broom," Danna suggested. "Taking action might help some of your worries fade."

"And some buckets, soap, and rags." Merritt fell into step beside her friend, passing through the doorway and out onto the boardwalk.

She squinted against the sun.

"How come I didn't know about your Jack?" Danna's words were spoken casually, but Merritt heard the undertone of hurt beneath.

Warmth tickled her neck and cheeks. "I thought of telling you so many times . . . "

Danna's sharp gaze made her flush intensify.

Why hadn't she? "I suppose . . . I suppose there was a part of me that didn't think he would go through with it."

Now Danna's brows drew tight with confusion. "Whyever not?"

"I am not exactly prime marriage material." She said it with a self-deprecating laugh so that the words would hurt less. "I'm not a young woman fresh from the schoolroom, dewy-eyed and naive."

One of Danna's brows rose in gentle humor. "Were you ever dewy-eyed?"

The marshal knew better.

"I'm independent and I know what I want. I speak my mind far too often and I'm—" She'd been going to say that she wasn't attractive enough to catch a husband in the traditional way.

But a memory popped into her mind. The way Jack had looked at her last night in the shadows and flickering light thrown by the fire. Like he'd wanted nothing more than to hold her close.

She hadn't felt average then. Or overlooked.

She'd felt . . . seen.

"Pssh." Danna made a dismissive sound, and Merritt blinked out of the memory as she stepped across a broken board.

Danna saw too much. "But he did show up. And he certainly seems interested in following through with the marriage."

Merritt thought of the way he'd strided beside her away from the wreckage—distance between them, hands dangling by their sides, not touching.

Of course, he must've been exhausted.

But she didn't think she was imagining the distance he'd put between them since he'd embraced her last night.

Had it felt as frightening to him as it had to her? The feeling of knowing someone so intimately while not really knowing them at all?

"You must be thinking I'm a fool to marry someone I barely know," Merritt said.

All the misgivings she'd felt building last night at supper writhed inside her like a coil of live snakes.

"If he's someone you could grow to love, what does it matter what I think? Or anyone else?"

Danna's matter-of-fact words hit with the force of a bludgeon.

Grow to love.

Merritt had been hoping for a friendly affection for Jack. Something calm and warm that would last years. A safe companion. The family she'd always wanted.

But when he'd held her last night, she'd felt the start of something so much bigger.

That felt more dangerous than anything else. What was she doing?

The cold wind bit into the skin of Merritt's exposed face, and she wrapped her scarf more tightly around her neck. And thought of Jack's hat. He'd given it away so easily.

"You overheard Mr. Polk this morning?" Danna asked.

Merritt nodded. "He wanted to be heard."

Danna frowned. "It didn't take much to discover where the fire started. The café had a fire in their kitchen last night. It was contained—Mrs. Steele thought it was out. But the wind was blowing straight toward the school, and some sparks must've carried over."

They'd had such a dry winter. The dusting of snow yesterday had been the first hint of moisture in weeks. It probably hadn't taken much for the wooden structure to catch fire.

"An accident," Merritt murmured.

"An accident."

Relief flooded her. She hadn't been negligent. But it was still a terrible reality that her students wouldn't have their school.

"I made a report to Mr. Polk and the other two board members," Danna continued, voice going low when they passed by the leather goods shop as someone was passing through the door.

"He wasn't happy?" Merritt asked.

"It was difficult to tell."

Merritt knew the man didn't like her. She also knew Danna had endured her own troubles with the town council two years ago when she had first become marshal.

"He hinted that the school board is unhappy that the pageant must be cancelled."

Merritt frowned. "I haven't even spoken to them yet." It'd only been hours since the cleanup. She'd been more focused on where the students would learn, how they would get supplies when the term began again.

"Will you have to argue to keep your job?" Danna asked.

The suggestion seemed absurd. Merritt had been schoolmarm in Calvin for more than eight years. She was an excellent teacher. She had signed a contract to teach through the end of the school year in May.

But Mr. Polk didn't like her. Maybe he had the power to convince Mr. Goodall and Mr. Beauchamp to end her contract early.

"I suppose it doesn't matter as much anymore," Danna said quietly as they approached the general store. "After you marry, you'll leave the classroom, right?"

Merritt shook her head. "I planned to stay through the spring, when my contract is up. They'll need that time to find a new teacher for fall." Though she had recently received a letter from her dear friend Darcy Weston that her younger sister Elsie might be looking for a teaching position.

Merritt thought of Clarissa and Samuel, Missy McCabe and Cody Billings. Even Daniel and Paul, who'd worked so hard to prepare for the pageant. Who had worked hard for recognition, to please their teacher.

She'd pushed Paul, knowing he had it in him to become a doctor or attorney if he worked hard enough.

She loved her students. And she wasn't going to simply walk away from them. She couldn't.

"If Mr. Polk still wants the pageant, we'll perform it," she said firmly. If her job was on the line, she'd give the town the best pageant ever performed. She wouldn't abandon the children, not at this juncture.

The warmth of the potbellied stove inside the store wafted over her and she loosened her scarf. Breathed in deeply.

"I'll make it happen somehow."

Piano music swelled. Smoke was heavy in the air, and there was carousing, arguing, and chatting, though it was quieter at the round table where Jack had sat down with two other men. At the bar, a woman in a skimpy purple dress lined with black lace leaned over the elbow of the nearest man.

There was a handful of coins in the center of the table. Jack didn't look at the cards face down on the table in front of him. He'd glanced at them once and memorized the cards before dropping them in front of him.

He was down a quarter so far, but that didn't worry him. Another hour or so and he'd win enough for a train ticket and to hold him over until after the holiday.

"I fold." The man with a bottlebrush mustache, across from Jack, tossed his cards on the table with a disgusted scowl.

"Same." The quiet, burly man with a scraggly dark beard tossed in his cards too.

Which left Jack to drag the pot toward himself.

Mustache collected the cards and started shuffling.

Jack watched his hands, always alert for shenanigans, though he'd be shocked if this man tried to sneak a card up his sleeve. Jack had been sitting across from him for an hour, and he was a slow thinker. He didn't have it in him to cheat.

The familiar sound of cards blitzing together should

have lit Jack up. He spent more time at a card table than anywhere else.

But tonight, the cigar smoke was irritating his eyes. The noise of that lonely cowboy doing an awful job of charming the saloon girl grated on his nerves. Even the feel of the cards under his fingers was off.

He couldn't stop thinking about those moments facing Merritt on the wide porch of the two-story boardinghouse. The words had been *right there* on his lips to tell her the truth, but the exhausted lines in her pretty face had dissuaded him. He couldn't do it.

He'd taken the coward's way out and agreed that they should meet for breakfast in the morning.

Except he'd seen the train schedule and knew there was an eastbound train leaving early in the morning.

He'd be on it. Gone from her life. Away from this town where he didn't belong.

It would be a good thing too. He couldn't forget that Morris had been on that train just yesterday. Some distance from that part of Jack's past wouldn't hurt.

Agitated, he tossed his cards down and folded. He'd lost track of the cards during this hand, a mistake he hadn't made since the early days when he'd started playing.

He told little white lies all the time. Being a little flexible with the truth was often a way to gain the good graces of someone Jack wanted to get closer to. It was part of how he was able to help people.

But something about speaking the lie to Merritt was bothering him like a pebble inside his boot.

He scratched the back of his neck, still missing his comfortable old cowboy hat. Straightened his shoulders and sat back in his chair a bit. He just needed to focus.

"Mind if I join in?" a new voice asked.

Jack vaguely recognized the man in a sharp vest and trousers and nodded a welcome. He'd met several folks and bumped elbows with a dozen others over the course of last night and this morning. He couldn't remember them all and only had a vague recollection of seeing this man before.

A new set of cards was dealt, and the antes were slid to the center of the table.

The new man flipped open the side of his jacket to reveal a fine vest underneath and a gold pocket watch dangling from inside. He placed a stack of dollar bills on the edge of the table.

He must've been sizing up Jack in the same way Jack had been doing, because his eyes narrowed.

"Do I know you? Ah. You're Miss Harding's beau."

Jack had kind of hoped to spend his hours here tonight avoiding any talk of Merritt. None of the other men in here had given any hint of recognition.

He picked up his cards for a glance and to keep from answering.

"Does she know you're here?" Pocket Watch pressed. He hadn't touched his cards yet. "She's such a sobersides—you can bet that once you're hitched, she won't allow for this kind of fun."

Scraggly Beard guffawed and Pocket Watch slapped his knee, amused at his own cleverness.

A thunderous anger stirred inside Jack. He didn't know

Merritt—not really—but he'd judged her as an upstanding woman. How dare these two mock her?

But there was a deeper part of him that knew Pocket Watch was right.

He couldn't imagine Merritt liking someone like him—the real him. The Jack who earned his living at a card table. It shouldn't matter. He was leaving in the morning.

You aren't playing against the man across the table. You're playing against yourself. Don't let your emotions get the better of you. Bybee's voice echoed in his mind.

The man had taught Jack everything he knew about cards. And then some. And that voice from his past was right.

Jack stuffed the anger down inside until all he felt was a cool indifference.

Even if he did feel a thrill of vindication when he won a total of two dollars off Pocket Watch.

He knew better than to press his luck or raise suspicion, so he pushed back his chair after the next hand.

Pocket Watch watched him with a baleful stare while Scraggly Beard and Mustache were busy counting their remaining funds and organizing the cards for the next hand.

Jack went out onto the boardwalk. Clouds had rolled in, though it wasn't snowing or raining. He stuffed his hands in his pockets. He'd won a little—not much more than he'd need for a train ticket.

He could go back in there. Something about Pocket Watch had tangled Jack's emotions. But with a few breaths of cold fresh air, he thought he could try again. Another couple of good pots and he'd be set for two weeks or more.

And he wouldn't mind lightening Pocket Watch's pocketbook after his insinuation about Merritt.

Several cowboys moseyed up the boardwalk, heading for the saloon. Jack trailed them inside.

But he quickly saw that the poker table had been abandoned. Jack settled in at the bar, scanning the room . . . There. Pocket Watch was nearby, partially blocked by two of the cowboys who'd bellied up to the bar. He was talking with another man in a sharp suit.

"It's a tragedy," the dark-suited man said. "A real shame." But his voice sounded gloating. "I would've burned down the school myself if I could've figured a way to do it without getting caught."

Jack froze. Who was that, and why was he talking about the school like that?

"Hey, boss!" the barman called out, waving a decanter of a golden-colored liquid, and the man in the sharp suit waved a hand at him. *Boss*? He might be the owner of the saloon.

He kept talking, unperturbed by the distraction. "Miss Harding has been a thorn in my side for months."

Pocket Watch fiddled with the squat glass on the table in front of him. "She's stubborner than an old mule. But the other two coots on the school board love her."

It clicked then, the connection that had been niggling in the back of Jack's mind since the man had sat down across the table. This was one of the men who made up the school board. Merritt's boss. He'd been at the site of the burnt building today.

The cowboy at Jack's side shifted, and Jack missed the

next part of what was said. Then, " . . . I'd love to have that parcel of land. Doesn't your cousin work for the land office?"

"Ernie? Yes, he does, but the deed for the school land belongs to the town."

The school land?

From his vantage point, half hidden behind the cowboy and trying not to give away that he was listening, Jack couldn't see the saloon owner's face. But he distinctly heard him say, "Pages can disappear from those record books."

What a slimy snake. How low would he sink to take away the school?

"The town council won't allow the town to be without a school for long," Pocket Watch said. "They'll rebuild. Somewhere else, maybe, if . . . ah . . . something happened to that deed."

"Think how much of a failure it'd be for her and the other church ladies if I built a saloon right across the street from their church."

Things began to clear up in Jack's mind. Merritt had turned her nose up at the saloon when they'd been walking to the restaurant that first night. *A thorn in my side for months.* It didn't take much imagination for him to picture Merritt rallying some of the mothers around town to protest the saloons. Cause what trouble she could.

And now this man wanted revenge for the slight.

"It's not enough," the saloon owner said, thumping his fist on the table. "I want her fired. Give her a reason to leave town."

Pocket Watch leaned closer, over the table. "I just played a coupla hands of poker with her mail-order fiancé."

The saloon owner perked up. "You don't say."

"I do say."

"I wonder what the other *church ladies*"—the words were spat with contempt—"would think about their prim and proper schoolmarm marrying a man of disrepute."

Pocket Watch laughed. "There's probably a paragraph in her teaching contract about maintaining an impeccable reputation."

Jack's temper sparked and he left quickly, pushing through the swinging doors and out into the night. He didn't hang around this time, didn't look up at the sky.

He was angry at the two men for their plotting—but also at himself.

He should've told Merritt the truth from the beginning. He hadn't thought his presence in town could hurt her, not when he would disappear so quickly. But the man he'd just played cards with had the power to mess with Merritt's job. Jack's mind whirled as he tried to come up with a solution. How could he make this problem go away for Merritt?

He thought of those kids, their bright eyes and eagerness to please the teacher they loved so much. He thought about Merritt. About the man who was supposed to have arrived on the train but had taken the coward's way out.

If Jack left now, the men plotting to take the tract of land and get Merritt fired would have free rein to do whatever they wanted. No one the wiser.

Merritt would be alone. Without a job. Those kids would be without a teacher.

It wasn't right.

And it was just the kind of problem Jack liked to solve. Men who thought they had power over others, who wanted to take something that wasn't theirs, thinking they had the right.

This problem wouldn't be solved by winning a few high-stakes hands at the poker table.

But was there another way?

Five

W HOA!"
The sound of a wagon creaking brought Merritt's head up from the checklist she held in one hand.

The sky was clear and she smiled at Will Chittim, who drove the empty wagon down the rutted street and into place just beside where she stood.

She glanced over her shoulder to see Jack in the open doorway of Mrs. Steele's restaurant. He was already carrying two straight-backed chairs, one in each arm, and moving through the doorway. His gaze glanced off hers, not holding.

There had been a few moments this morning as she'd been readying for the day when she'd feared that Jack wouldn't meet her for breakfast. Even so, she'd spent a few extra minutes getting her hair just right in the looking glass.

He'd seen her a crying, sooty mess just the night before.

Certainly that wasn't the put-together, well-mannered woman he'd come here to find.

She'd woken from a deep sleep—a dream she couldn't remember—with the terrible cramp in her stomach telling her he was gone. That he'd decided against marrying her after all.

But when she'd opened her front door to walk down to the café as they'd planned, he'd been there, standing on the path with his back turned to her door, staring at the house across the street.

She'd felt such a shock of joy at seeing him—and attraction when she'd realized he'd shaved the scruff from his handsome jawline—that she'd covered it by ducking her head shyly.

Their breakfast had been interrupted by Cody Billings, one of her students, who'd apparently been all over town looking for Merritt. The boy had rushed into the café, his hair windblown and mittens flying, to tell Merritt that the restaurant owner wanted her to use the tables and chairs for the interim school until the kitchen stove in the restaurant could be repaired.

Merritt and Jack had cut their breakfast short so that Merritt could oversee everything being moved into the dance hall. That had been about two hours ago.

Jack shuffled past her now with his arms full of chairs. Behind him came Mr. Carson, the preacher, also with his arms full, and the man's two teenaged children, each with a chair.

Will had hopped from the wagon seat into the back and was reaching for each chair as it was handed up to him.

Jack was the first to give up his burden, and he came to stand next to her, arms crossed over his chest.

"This is the last load," she told him. The morning had been spent wrangling wagons and moving furniture. "If Mrs. Quinn and Mrs. Billings are finished sweeping out the dance hall, I can arrange the tables and chairs and perhaps I could feed you lunch at my house. I can meet you there—it's not necessary—I'm sure you have other things to do than carting around furniture."

He didn't look away from where Cyrus Carson was handing his chair into the wagon. "It'd be better if we ate at the café." Jack slid a glance her direction. "Better for your reputation."

She flushed. "We're to be married in a few days. Surely having lunch together isn't inappropriate."

His eyes shadowed and a muscle in his cheek jumped.

The Carsons excused themselves. Merritt waved as they moved down the boardwalk.

"You want a lift over to the dance hall?" Will called out.

She thought she would rather walk next to Jack for the few blocks.

"Love one," Jack said before she could decline. He extended his hand for her to go first, and she didn't want to be rude.

She accepted his hand up into the wagon seat. With her next to Will, there was nowhere for Jack to sit.

She was prepared to get back down, not wanting to leave her fiancé behind. Jack seemed to read the intention in her expression, because he shook his head slightly. "I'll walk."

Will leaned forward and spoke to Jack. "You can step up on the brake bar and hold the side of the box. It isn't far."

Jack took a step back and jumped up onto something she couldn't see beneath the wagon box, clinging to the side.

Will was already clucking the horse into motion.

"Isn't that dangerous?" A gust of wind blew her papers, and she pressed them to her bosom to keep them from flying away. Her seat felt precarious as she twisted to try and see Jack.

"Only if he falls," Will said from behind her.

Her heart thumped, but it was the pirate's grin Jack sent her that made her pulse begin to race.

"I used to do this all the time when I was a boy. With my brother."

There was a look of boyish joy in his expression. The wind ruffled his hair, and she remembered that he'd given his hat away yesterday.

The wagon wheels must've hit a rut, and she bounced on the spring seat, one hand letting go of her papers to clutch the bench beneath her. Jack whooped with delight.

She shook her head.

"Almost there," Will murmured.

They pulled up in front of the dance hall, and Will set the brake.

Jack was already there to help her down. She'd climbed in and out of wagons her entire life, but today her foot slipped on the wheel spoke as she used it for a step down.

Jack's strong arm banded around her waist as he caught her against himself.

"All right?"

She was caught in his dark-eyed gaze, trapped in the intensity so that she couldn't breathe—

"All right, Miss Harding?" That was Will's voice, and it broke her from the frozen state.

She stepped back from Jack, brushing off her skirts with one hand while still holding her papers with the other. She cleared her throat. "Yes."

Jack was still, his eyes hooded.

"I didn't know you had a brother," she blurted. "You didn't write about him in your letters."

His expression went carefully blank. "He passed away years ago."

Will had jumped into the back of the wagon, and Jack brushed past Merritt to reach for one of the chairs the young man was handing down. Jack placed it carefully on the boardwalk and then reached for another one.

Merritt rushed inside and dropped her papers on the nearest table, then went back outside to help.

She bumped Jack out of the way to take the next chair from Will.

"What was he like?" she asked over her shoulder. "Your brother? What was his name?"

He didn't meet her eyes as they changed places. She couldn't help but notice the way the muscles of his shoulder rippled beneath his coat.

He didn't answer, and she reached for the next chair.

"Jack?" she prompted. Perhaps she bumped his arm on purpose when she next passed.

He shook himself, as if he'd been lost in his memories. "His name was Dewey. He was only eleven when he died."

His voice had gone gruff, and her heart squeezed to hear the grief in his tone. He obviously still missed his brother.

"What was he like?" she asked again. "What kind of person was he? Charming and kind, like you?"

His eyes flicked to hers and held for a moment before he took the last chair from her hands and added it to their haphazard stack on the boardwalk.

"He was an old soul. Could sing or hum a tune even if he only heard it once. He was always whistling something. Used to drive me crazy."

But the affectionate tone in his voice belied the statement.

"You want help carrying them in?" Will asked from the wagon box.

She realized he was waiting to go. "We can do it," she told Will. "You've been a big help this morning. I'm sure you're hungry."

He nodded and hopped back onto the wagon seat.

Jack had already started carrying two of the chairs toward the open door of the dance hall.

She tried to pick up two but found it cumbersome with her skirts, so she grabbed one with both hands and began to follow him.

"What about your parents?" she called out after him, huffing a bit as she attempted to keep up with his long-legged stride. "I know your mother passed away. Is your father well?"

He dropped the two chairs to the floor with a clatter, though they didn't fall.

The window of the dance hall sent a rectangle of light

against the shadows inside. Jack stood just behind it, his face in shadow. "I don't want to talk about my family."

She was trembling a little as he brushed past her, and she was left to put her chair around one of the round tables that had been moved inside.

She hadn't meant to pry, and she told him so as he met her in the doorway, already carrying two more chairs through.

"I thought . . . I just wanted to get to know you better," she said softly. "We've only exchanged the few letters. I-I'm sorry if I pushed too hard."

She couldn't read his expression, but he didn't quite meet her eyes. "We'll talk. Later."

She ducked outside, the bright sunlight stinging her eyes in contrast to the darkened inside of the building.

When she passed back inside and he grunted that he'd get the last two chairs, she was left to look at her list. But her eyes were watering and she couldn't quite focus.

She wanted to know Jack. She'd thought he would want that too.

But perhaps she was being too forward. She hadn't expected this prickly side of him.

She didn't know how to smooth things over.

"We brung lunch!"

The childish voice called out just before the noise of several pairs of feet tromped through the door.

Jack looked up from where he'd stationed himself in the middle of the tables. Merritt was standing near the door, poring over several papers in her hands.

They'd passed several minutes in silence.

He'd hurt her with his curt response to her question about his parents. She was too easy to read—wasn't hiding her emotions at all—and he'd seen the quick blink and the hurt in her eyes before she'd ducked her head over those papers.

He was sorry for it.

There was a part of him that wanted her to look at him the way she had yesterday, like he was some hero.

Except he wasn't.

And he'd realized, when she'd mentioned the letters, that he didn't know what the real John had told her about himself. Jack was already deceiving her, letting her believe he was the groom she'd been waiting for. He didn't want to lie to her face.

And talking about Dewey had brought back the rawness of his memories of that time. Jack's childhood was something he'd rather forget. Not talk about. He'd been raised in an orphanage in Chicago and put on a train at the age of eleven. The benefactors from the big city had hoped that the children they'd sent west would find loving homes.

But that hadn't happened for Jack. He would never call the people who'd taken him in Ma and Pa.

And he was certain Merritt didn't want to know about them.

The interruption was welcome. Merritt glanced his way with a guarded gaze before turning to greet the handful of children that scampered inside followed by several mothers and a woman in pants with a silver star on her chest.

Jack hid a scowl. He might be telling a white lie by letting

Merritt believe he was her intended groom, but he'd never had an affinity for the law. Not after a small-town deputy had refused to help him and Dewey.

"Nothing is clean," Merritt protested as the children displayed picnic baskets they'd brought with them.

"We brung blankets!" one of the boys said gleefully.

"Brought blankets," Merritt corrected idly.

"C'mon and eat, Mr. Jack!" The same little girl who'd been so upset yesterday morning, the very one he'd given his blanket to, waved him over.

How could he say no? He found himself kneeling on the edge of her blanket. Another girl had tugged Merritt over by the hand. Merritt glanced warily at Jack before she sat beside him, then arranged her skirt around her legs. Was it to keep from looking at him?

"Sorry for the interruption," the young mother muttered aside to Merritt as the two girls dug in the picnic blanket. "I know you're trying to clean up and arrange things, but they were going stir-crazy, and we wanted to find out whether we could help."

"It's fine," Merritt said graciously. "I'm not sure how much more I—we—can do without books or slates."

"How're we going to rehearse for the pageant without our lines?" a boy of ten called out from another blanket. He had a chicken leg in one hand, and his chin was smeared with grease.

"Miss Harding has the whole thing memorized," the older of the little girls on Jack's blanket piped up, sounding exasperated. "She wrote it, anyway."

Jack slanted a glance at Merritt. "You wrote the pageant script?"

Here was another stark difference between them. She was whip-smart, while he could barely read, and that had been self-taught.

Pink roses appeared high on her cheeks. "It's mostly from the Bible."

The mother from the next blanket teased, "I don't remember a talking donkey in the biblical account."

Merritt pulled a face. "Every child needs at least a few words."

"Oh, I understand. My Tobias is thrilled to have a speaking part."

The mother from Jack's blanket stopped her littlest girl from putting a glob of mashed potatoes on her sister's skirt. "Do you remember when Merritt wrote that serial story when we were . . . oh, I was ten. You must've been thirteen."

Now Merritt had ducked her head. He couldn't seem to look away from the two women.

"She won the county spelling bee two years running," the other woman said.

"Can't forget the time she wrangled all four of her cousins into that Easter play," one of the mothers farther away in the cavernous space called over. "Remember Isaac as the ox, pulling that pony cart?"

"Nothing to be embarrassed about," the mother on his blanket said, patting Merritt's arm.

Merritt looked up and that wrinkle above her nose was standing out. "I'm not embarrassed," she said coolly.

"God made you to be a teacher. And a fine one," the woman said.

But he felt the stillness that had come over her.

"Are you gonna have kids after you get married?" the young girl asked.

Jack coughed up the bit of biscuit he'd just swallowed.

Merritt didn't seem to be paying attention to him as she answered calmly, "I've always wanted a big family." She cut a glance to him. "Of course, you already know that."

John did, wherever the man was. But Jack simply stowed the knowledge away.

Not for you, Jack's mind whispered.

Here was another obstacle that meant they were never supposed to be a pair in the first place. He'd always known he'd have a solitary future—moving from one town to the next, setting wrongs to right.

Merritt was obviously a fixture in this town. She'd grown up here. Had roots. And she wanted a big family.

He had no idea what it meant to be a good father. He'd had no example of one growing up.

It was good that he was leaving. The sooner, the better.

A shadow passed through the open doorway, and he looked up to see a young woman and a twenty-something man enter. He recognized the young man, Albert Hyer. Jack had met him at the general store, working behind the counter earlier this morning when Jack had knocked on the still-locked doors just after sunup.

A little girl got up off one of the farthest blankets and ran to embrace the young woman. Hyer's wife?

"We brought some supplies," Hyer announced. "They're just outside."

There was a stampede as most of the children abandoned their blankets and food to go see.

Merritt stood up and moved to talk to the young woman. A loving glance passed between Hyer and his sweetheart before he moved in Jack's direction.

Jack stood up and moved away from the blanket—and ears that might be listening.

The young man stuck out his hand for Jack to shake, and Jack took it. "We had everything you wanted except for the blue paint."

Jack shot a look over the kids' shoulders, trying to make sure they weren't in earshot. "It's fine. I told you—"

"Oh, yeah." Hyer looked sheepish.

"Miss Harding! It's supplies for the pageant backdrops!"

Children were filing in. Some of them were dragging a bolt of white canvas, some carrying paintbrushes or jars of paint.

The boys and girls were beaming, each face lit up like it was Christmas morning. Or at least, what Jack imagined a Christmas morning would be like.

He found himself idly ruffling the back of his hair before he dropped his arm.

"They sure are happy about it. How come you want it to be a secret that you bought all that stuff?" Hyer asked. Jack had spent the two bucks he'd won at the poker table last night but felt lighter.

Jack turned a serious look on the kid. "Because that's the way I want it."

Merritt was squatting down, nodding along with a girl who was speaking animatedly. Her face had lost some of the worry lines bracketing her mouth.

That was all the thanks he needed.

"You know Ernie Duff?" he asked the kid.

"Uh . . . he works for the land office." Hyer shrugged and moved off to join his young wife. Jack hoped the kid hadn't told her.

"You looking to buy a parcel of land?"

Jack turned his head, trying not to show his surprise as the marshal sidled up next to him. He hadn't realized she'd been that close. His chest locked up a little, but he worked to maintain a calm exterior.

"No," he said. The saloon owner had said Duff could interfere with the land deed for the parcel of land the school was built on. Jack needed to know more about the man. Did he take bribes? Pocket Watch was his cousin.

"Buying a house, then? Or got your eye on a farm nearby?"

The marshal was sharp. He could tell by the intelligent look in her eyes that she didn't miss much. She stood with hands casually on her hips, but alert and watchful.

"No. I just heard the name. Trying to make sense of who's who in town."

She didn't call his bluff. Her eyes skittered to Merritt and back to Jack.

"She's independent, but she's got a tender heart. You'll do well to treat her right."

His hackles went up. Was the marshal threatening him? Or simply trying to protect her friend?

"I would never want to hurt her," he said, gaze drawn back to Merritt.

Merritt was directing the children where to stack the supplies, and for a moment, he caught her looking back at him. She was smiling, and a wisp of hair had fallen loose from her bun, lying against her cheek.

I would never want to hurt her.

So what was he still doing here?

Six

A BRISK WIND WAS BLOWING AS MER-
ritt stepped out of the dance hall, Jack accompanying
her. She secured the door carefully behind her.

Twila and Albert Hyer had been the last ones out, and
now they remained on the boardwalk, Albert shaking Jack's
hand.

"Thank you for coming out," Merritt said. "You truly
don't have any idea who donated the supplies?" She felt
uneasy that she didn't know whom to thank.

"I truly don't." Twila smiled. "Albert wouldn't tell me."
She paused. "I couldn't help noticing the way your Jack
looks at you. Like he's never seen something so fine and
he can't believe it's his."

Merritt shook her head, cheeks blazing. "He doesn't."
She darted a look in the men's direction and thankfully
found them in conversation. Jack didn't seem to have heard.

I don't want to talk about that.

Jack had been closed off, though he'd worked side by side with her all afternoon.

"Hmm. I suppose you might've missed those looks, as busy as you've been all day. But I saw."

Twila looked happier than Merritt had ever seen her. Even when a gust of wind blasted them, Twila only tightened her wrap around herself and smiled as she turned to face Merritt more directly.

"Albert thinks we should wait, but I know you'll understand why I have to share . . . We are in the family way."

It took a moment and a blink for Merritt to make sense of the rapidly spoken words. And then she was embracing her former student—one of the first young ladies who'd graduated from her schoolroom—and whispering congratulations in her ear.

Albert wore a look of both consternation and adoration as he took his young wife's arm and steered her away toward the general store and their rooms above it.

And Merritt was left with Jack. Who did not take her arm as she faced into the wind to walk home.

She ducked her face into her scarf. "I'll make supper," she said resolutely.

He didn't say anything to that as he fell into step beside her, heading toward her bungalow. Thankfully it wasn't far.

He glanced over his shoulder, the way the young couple had gone. "You seem close with Twila."

Merritt stepped over a slushy bit between the two buildings, where the boardwalk ended with a set of three stairs.

"Believe it or not, she was a pill when I first became the teacher here."

His boots clonked on the boardwalk as they took the next set of steps. "And you won her over?"

Merritt chuckled a little, remembering those days. "It took almost the entire first year."

"Because she was stubborn?"

"Because I had no idea how to corral a classroom of students. It took time to discover that some children learn differently from others, that some need a soft touch while others need strong leadership."

He glanced at her, and she wanted to believe that was admiration in his gaze. They left the boardwalk behind, and her shoes crunched in the icy mud of the street that led back to Merritt's home.

"Twila is actually the reason I answered your ad," Merritt said when the silence had lengthened.

"You took advice from a youngster?" He sounded so appalled that she laughed.

"Certainly not. She invited me to her wedding." Merritt remembered sitting in the pew after Sunday services, along with most of the townsfolk, watching Twila say her vows to Albert. She'd been absolutely beaming, and all Merritt could think was, *I want to feel like that*.

"I've always wanted a family," she told him as they walked through a patch of shadows thrown by the sun setting behind a house across the street. "Felt like I had plenty of time to find a husband and settle down."

Her stomach twisted, an echo of what she'd felt as she'd watched Twila cling to Albert's arm as they skated down the aisle.

"Seeing one of my students all grown up and starting

a family of her own was the push I needed," she said. "A reminder that time was slipping away. I love my students," she said quickly. "But I started to feel as if I could disappear into the schoolmarm for all time."

He was quiet for a moment, the only noises their breathing and the crunch of their footsteps.

"I heard someone say the school board won't allow you to teach after you marry," he said finally. "Will you be happy not being in the classroom?"

She had written the answer in one of her letters. Didn't he remember? She wasn't sure where the disappointment that she swallowed came from.

"I'm sure I'll find purpose and keep busy once we start our family." Saying the words aloud brought a rush of warmth to her cheeks, quickly doused by the cold.

He didn't look at her.

They were almost home now, and she heard the blow of a horse—there were children standing at her front door, waiting. Her heart leaped in recognition, though these bodies weren't from her classroom.

And three tall men stood in almost-identical poses on the small patch of grass in front of her house, another shorter form in shadow behind them.

"Drew! Ed! Nick! What are you doing here?"

Two girlish forms darted toward her. Fourteen-year-old David hung back with his father and uncles. Merritt braced her feet as she caught Tillie in one arm and Jo in the other. "Hello, you two. I'm so glad to see you!" She hugged them close, noting how tall Jo was getting. Almost to her chin now.

"We heard there was a fire at the school!" Jo said.

"Are you hurt?" Tillie asked, leaning back to peer at Merritt.

David had left the stoop to come forward, and he gave her a hug from the side in the spot where Jo had just vacated. "Hi, Merry." David had given her the nickname when he was a toddler and it had stuck.

Tillie still clung to her side as Merritt said, "I'm fine. It happened at night, when no one was at the building."

Tillie didn't seem convinced. "You wasn't there?"

"I wasn't inside," Merritt said, popping a kiss on the girl's forehead.

Jack had gone still next to her at the onslaught of children approaching. When she looked in his direction, she caught Drew and Ed with their arms crossed over their chests, taking Jack's measure.

"Who's that?" Tillie asked. The child was innately curious.

Merritt finally disengaged from the girl to step back next to Jack. She slipped her arm through his, felt his tension in the way he held himself.

"Jack, these are my cousins. I wrote you about them. This is Jack," she said determinedly. "My fiancé."

Jo's eyes went wide, while Tillie gasped—"Yer gettin' married?"

In the flurry of introductions, Nick, the youngest of the four McGraw brothers, was the first to step forward. "Nick McGraw. Happy to meet you."

Jack reached forward and met Nick's handshake, but Merritt still had hold of his other arm and couldn't help noticing that his tension hadn't eased at the welcoming gesture.

She left his side and went to Drew and Ed. They were standing close enough that she could throw her arms around both of them. "Stop that," she chided them. "You're not changing my mind, so you might as well say hello."

Ed's crossed arms fell loose first as her normally easy-going cousin patted her back with one hand.

Drew took a moment longer, but then he relaxed his stance, too, and hugged her shoulders before moving to shake Jack's hand.

"I suppose you all are hungry. Come inside and I'll start frying up some ham."

The kids didn't need a second invitation. They tromped inside like a herd of cattle. Ed followed, eyebrows raised in delight.

Jack hung back and she moved to his side while Drew and Nick were still standing nearby.

"They're not a bad bunch once you get to know them."

Jack looked to the side, giving his profile momentarily. "You should spend the time with your family," he said in a low voice.

She'd expected there to be hiccups, she reminded herself. But not for family to be one of them.

"They'll be your family in a few days too," she reminded him. "Come inside."

He looked like he would argue with her, but she flicked her eyes to Drew, who was watching them intently.

"Didn't Isaac want to come?" she asked, feigning innocence. "Since you were all worried about me after the fire."

Her oldest cousin had the grace to look abashed, while Nick hid a grin by turning his head.

"Isaac's up at the winter cabin," Drew muttered. "Someone has to watch the cattle."

It was unspoken, but she knew that Isaac was having a difficult time since he'd come home from his last job with the US Marshals months ago. He'd been closemouthed about what had happened—she wasn't sure even Drew knew what had sent him home from the job he'd loved—and he rarely came to town.

She saw Drew's gaze flick behind her just before she felt the warmth of Jack's hand clasping hers. His tall form sidled next to her.

It wouldn't do for him to return to the boardinghouse hungry. Relieved, she gave a tug on his hand and pulled him toward the house.

She'd set Tillie on him. Tillie could charm the meanest hen in the henhouse. Jack wouldn't stand a chance.

Jack didn't know what he'd expected the inside of Merritt's home to look like, but her front room was simple and neat. Two small sofas were kitty-corner on two walls, a low table between them. One entire wall was taken up with a floor-to-ceiling shelf, and it was full to bursting with books. There were even stacks of books beneath the table and on the floor next to the bookcase.

Beyond the sitting room was a tiny hallway to a closed door that he assumed was her bedroom, and past the hall, a doorway that led to the kitchen. The door was open and he could see a small flowerpot on the kitchen windowsill.

Merritt had abandoned him.

At least, she'd excused herself to the kitchen to cook supper. He'd heard the clank of pans, the crackle of kindling taking hold in the stove. The two girls had gone with her. David and Nick had gone to settle the horses and wagon at the livery for the night.

Which left Jack in the room with Drew and Ed.

"Where did you say you were from?"

Drew had asked the question, but Ed's intense gaze was a mirror of his brother's.

"Here and there." Jack still didn't know what John-the-groom had written in his letters, didn't know how much Merritt had told her cousins about her potential groom.

"What happened to your hat? Hey, Merry," Drew called into the kitchen, "I'm not sure I can trust a guy without a hat!"

"Lost it," Jack said cheerfully. "How far's your ranch?"

It must be pretty far if they were staying the night in town. The oldest brother had mentioned staying in the bunkhouse of a rancher nearby. The girls would stay the night here with their cousin, *Merry*.

Drew stared at him.

It was Ed that answered. "About half a day's ride."

"How many cattle you run?"

If he could keep the conversation focused on the brothers, it'd make everything simpler.

"Almost a hundred head," Drew answered. "You got family back home?"

Jack sat down on the sofa, crossing one ankle over his knee. "No family. Why do you want to know?"

Drew's eyes narrowed. "Wondering whether you're going to try to take Merritt away from her family."

They'll be your family in a few days. Merritt's words from moments ago whispered through his mind.

They wouldn't. He knew it.

And it seemed Drew wasn't too keen on the idea of this match.

Merritt appeared in the kitchen doorway. The scent of frying ham had his mouth watering. The sounds of something sizzling on the stove were muted, as were the girls' voices behind her.

"We'll be staying in Calvin long enough for me to finish the school year," she told her cousin primly. "Not that it's your business."

She set several tin coffee mugs on the table with a clank. The pot followed with a heavier clunk.

"You can pour, Ed," she said. She pointed a finger at Drew. "Be nice."

There'd been a flurry of introductions outside, and the young girl he thought was named Tillie skipped into the room, carrying a glass of milk. There'd been no mention of a mother. Was Drew widowed? Jack's curiosity was piqued, despite knowing he should ignore those thoughts.

"What're you doing, peanut?" Drew asked as she skirted him and then came to sit right next to Jack on the sofa.

"Merry asked me to come rescue Mr. Jack." She took a sip of her milk and set her cup on the table too. She had a small milk mustache across her upper lip, and it made her look innocent somehow.

He felt another kick in his stomach. Had Dewey ever been as innocent as this girl seemed?

Her leg swung where her foot didn't touch the floor. "What d'you need rescuin' for, Mr. Jack?"

He glanced up to where Ed had turned his smile into his shoulder and Drew was staring at him. "I reckon I don't."

She tipped her head to one side. "Then how come Merry thinks so? She's real smart, ya know? If she says you need rescuin', ya prob'ly do."

She said the words with such earnestness that he couldn't argue. But Merritt was wrong. He didn't need rescuing from these men. He could hold his own at a card table with men more dangerous than these. Men with loaded weapons in their laps. He wouldn't be afraid of her family.

Tillie pointed toward a small pile of brown-wrapped packages in one corner of the room, half hidden behind the edge of the sofa. He hadn't noticed them until now.

"Those're our Christmas presents." Tillie whispered so loudly that the sound carried across the room. "Merry always gets me a book, but this year I'm hopin' for a dolly."

His lips twitched with the urge to smile. "You'll be as smart as your cousin if you read lots of books," he said.

The girl wrinkled her nose. "I cain't read yet."

From across the room, Drew grunted. "We're too far out for the kids to attend school in town." If Jack wasn't mistaken, there was a flush of guilt in his expression.

Nick and David stomped inside, complaining that the wind was turning colder. The added bodies and noise

turned the attention off Jack and filled the room fair to
bursting.

Soon enough, Jack found himself seated at the round
table in one corner of Merritt's kitchen, surrounded by the
children, his knee pressed against Merritt's.

"How come you haven't decorated for Christmas?" Tillie
asked, her mouth full.

"I supposed I haven't had time this year," Merritt said
with a furtive glance at Jack. "I've been extra busy with
the pageant."

And if he'd learned anything about her at all the past two
days, he suspected she'd be up late tonight writing down
the pageant script.

"They're not still going to hold it?" Nick said from across
the room, where he stood at the counter with his plate.

Merritt nodded. "We are. At the dance hall."

Nick commiserated with her, and Jack learned that he'd
once wanted to become a teacher. Again, Jack's curiosity
was engaged. Why was the young man back on the ranch
instead of following his passion?

The family camaraderie was evident when Tillie spilled
her cup of milk and David helped her mop it up. Jo rolled
her eyes, but he also saw the girl sneak a piece of her biscuit
onto Tillie's plate when the girl complained of still being
hungry.

Drew and Nick ribbed Ed about the wooden top he'd
promised to craft his nephew for Christmas and promptly
forgotten about.

Merritt was teased for keeping her mail-order beau a

secret, but she took it with good-natured laughter, nudging his boot with her shoe beneath the table.

Jack knew every move to make at the poker table. How to present himself, how to hold his cards and arrange his chips to let his confidence shine through.

But in the middle of a family supper like this . . . he was completely out of his element. He soaked it all in, listening and watching and staying out of it as much as he could.

And then he found himself on dishes duty, prompted by Tillie, who claimed it was her turn to be rescued from the mountain of dishes.

He was elbow-deep in sudsy water and she was standing on a chair beside him, drying, when she said, "I like you, Mr. Jack."

He only hesitated a moment. "I like you too." It was impossible not to. The young girl was full of stories about her room, her uncle's dog, and the ranch.

"I'm glad you came here to marry Merry." The girl giggled at the rhyming words. "Now you'll be in our family forever."

He couldn't answer that. His throat was hot.

"How'd you learn how to be a businessman?"

He cleared his throat, thankful for her quick mind that had already taken her in another direction.

Tillie continued, "I don't know what I want to do when I grow up. Maybe be a teacher like Merry."

How he'd learned to gamble wasn't a story for a little girl. But she was watching him with curious, focused eyes, and he knew she was waiting for an answer.

He glanced over his shoulder. Merritt and her cousins

and the other kids had gone into the front room. The adults were drinking coffee, and Jack could hear two of the brothers arguing about something.

"For a while, I didn't know what I wanted to do. I lost my parents . . . and was alone for a long time." He stumbled through the story, trying to edit as he spoke. There were parts a little girl shouldn't know.

He'd been aimless after he'd run away from the Farrs' farm. He'd wanted to get as far away as possible. He'd taken odd jobs. Helped with harvest in a nearby small town.

"And then I met a friend of mine. Bybee. He taught me his trade." Playing cards. "Realized I had a knack for it. Taught me everything he knew."

Unfortunately, Bybee hadn't been as naturally talented or skilled as Jack. He'd cheated one too many times and been caught. There'd been a brawl, guns drawn. Jack's mentor and only friend had been gone with a flash of light and the echoing *bang!* from a revolver. Jack hadn't had time to mourn; he'd had to move on quickly lest someone accuse him of being a part of Bybee's cheating.

"We . . . ah . . . had to part ways," he told Tillie as he handed her the last plate. "But I never forgot what he taught me." How to read tells, having the patience to strike at the right moment.

Tillie dried the plate with her tongue sticking out of the corner of her mouth. She was adorable, and Jack's heart panged.

Before long, the McGraws took their leave. Drew carried a sleepy Tillie on his shoulder out the door, the last one to go.

Jack should be going himself. He hadn't missed the flick of a curtain across the street and knew that Merritt's neighbors might be watching Jack's comings and goings. He didn't want to risk her reputation—more than he already had.

Tonight, being with her and the family had shown him a different kind of life. He was used to being on his own, leaving a saloon after a late night and sometimes lying on a random hotel bed in his clothes, staring up at the ceiling before he was able to drift off. He had never wanted evenings like tonight.

That wasn't true. There was still a part of a little boy inside him, one who had ridden west on a train with other orphans, who had hoped for a family just like this.

It hurt to remember.

Merritt had taken the coffee mugs into the kitchen and was returning as he shrugged into his coat.

"I'd better go."

She looked surprised, but then her glance flicked to the window. "It *is* late, I suppose."

Merritt watched him for a moment that stretched long. "You aren't what I expected from your letters. I heard you talking with Tillie. Why didn't you tell me about losing both of your parents?"

He didn't want to lie to her. "That's in the past."

"It's still a part of you," she said softly.

Tillie had got the information out of him, almost too easily. Where was the man who could hold his own against sharp poker players?

"You can trust me with your true self," she said.

He touched his temple, only then remembering that he was missing a hat. He stepped out into the cold night without answering her.

Merritt didn't know who he really was.

She had some picture of him in mind, a picture of that John fellow from the train.

That wasn't the real Jack. The real Jack had an ugly past. Had hired guns trying to track him down.

If there was one thing he knew, it was that someone like Merritt—a smart, beautiful woman, respected in her community and loved by her family—would never end up with someone like him.

If she knew the real Jack, she would judge him worthless. Just like Mrs. Farr had.

Seven

T HE SUN WAS BARELY UP WHEN DREW found Jack at the site of the fire.

"Want to tell me what you're doin'?" Drew asked.

"Not particularly." Jack sliced the shovel into the debris with a *snick*.

He'd shed his coat a half hour ago. He had a borrowed shovel in hand, and a borrowed lamp sat conspicuously on a two-foot-high stump of wood, though Jack had doused it when the morning light had become bright enough to see. It had taken a good two hours, but he'd managed to scrape one corner free of charred chunks of wood and debris all the way down to the dirt.

It was grubby work. Ash stuck to his clothes and face where he'd worked up a sweat. He felt gross compared to Drew's clean clothes, though the rancher's were worn with age.

"Went lookin' for you at the boardinghouse," Drew said.

He had a coffee tin in hand, and Jack's nose twitched at the scent of coffee. It was a welcome relief after the acrid soot he'd been breathing in.

"Mrs. Stoll was surprised you weren't in your room. She did say you came in at a reasonable hour last night."

Jack grimaced. What did Merritt's cousin want? He could only hope that the gossip mill left it alone, didn't believe he'd snuck out to go to Merritt.

"You look thirsty," Drew said when Jack stuck the shovel into the ground to lift a chunk of burnt log into the empty wagon a few steps away. He'd already nearly filled it up, planning to move the debris away from the site.

Jack slapped the dust off his hands and looked at Drew. "What do you want?"

Drew shrugged. "Just lookin' for you."

Jack stared at him. The other man didn't have an obvious tell—he'd noticed that last night—but looked a little worn around the edges. "I figured you'd have brought both your brothers if you meant to run me off."

Drew sipped his coffee, his hand steady. "Who said anything about runnin' you off?"

It became a stalemate as they stared at each other.

Finally, Drew relented, a small smile pulling at one side of his lips. "Here."

He held out the tin cup from his other side. Jack accepted it warily. He *was* thirsty. His mouth tasted of grit and ash, and he gulped the liquid. The coffee must've grown cold while Drew had been looking for him, but the drink was still welcome.

"Want to tell me why you're sneaking around for this

cleanup?" Drew asked, surveying what Jack had already done. "Folks'll look more kindly on you if they actually see you doing the work."

Jack took another drink. "I don't care about that."

Drew glanced at him from the corner of his eye. "You don't."

His words weren't a clear question, but Jack shrugged. It was true. Merritt had told him last night that the local preacher expected to meet with him later. He had no plans to attend that meeting and figured that working out here was as good an excuse as any to skip the meeting. No doubt the man would preach fire and brimstone at him, like Mr. Farr had. No thanks.

In the distance, the train whistle blew. Jack knew the schedule, knew it was pulling into town soon.

Jack kept assessing Drew as he swigged the last of the coffee. Merritt's cousin was an upstanding man. It was there in the quiet questions he'd asked last night when he'd thought no one else would hear. Checking on her, asking what she needed after the fire. It was obvious he loved Merritt and was protective of her.

Jack lowered the coffee tin to his side. "Do you know Ernie Duff?"

Drew's brow wrinkled. "From the land office? I know of him. Why?"

Jack worked alone. Had ever since Bybee had been killed. But he didn't know the people in town like Drew did, and instinct told him that Drew was just as upstanding as Merritt.

He gulped the last of the coffee and put the tin on the

corner of the wagon seat nearby. "The other night, I heard a coupla men talking about the schoolhouse and Merritt's job."

Drew's eyes narrowed. "Who?"

"One of them was a school board member. Another one seemed like he owned the saloon."

"Billy Burns." Drew squinted even harder, and Jack wanted to quail under his direct attention but he showed nothing. "He's friendly with Polk—one of the school board members. How'd you have occasion to overhear a conversation between them?"

What were you doing in that saloon? That's what he meant.

But Jack didn't have to answer that.

"Seems like Burns wants this chunk of land." Jack jerked his thumb toward the mess of ash and debris. "Something about getting revenge on the church ladies? Merritt especially."

Drew rolled his eyes. "There's a couple of busybodies in town that would love to close down every saloon. I've told Merritt to stay clear of it, but . . . " He shrugged.

Jack had guessed right.

"Burns and his accomplice were cooking up a plan that, if rebuilding the school took long enough, maybe this Duff character could lose the deed that says the school belongs to the town."

"And Burns could buy it," Drew said grimly. He tipped his head to the site. "That's why you're out here?"

Jack didn't answer him directly. "Burns said he'd help make sure the schoolmarm didn't keep her job."

Something kept Jack from saying the rest—that Jack's presence in that saloon and in town was damaging her reputation.

He'd done his duty. He'd told Drew. Drew would help. He lifted the shovel and trudged back into the ash.

But Drew followed him, the sound of his steps quiet where everything had been trampled down. "Wait a minute."

Jack felt a line of tension stretch across his shoulders. He dug the shovel into the ash and began to move it aside, clearing down to the pure dirt underneath.

"What does it matter if Merritt loses her job? I thought y'all getting married meant she'd be finished in the classroom."

Jack kept shoveling, but Drew grabbed his shoulder and hauled Jack around to face him. Jack dropped the shovel with a thunk. He straightened, chest puffing out, hands curling into fists at his sides.

The train whistle tooted two short blasts. Pulling out now. Jack should've been on it. He knew it.

"You planning on marrying my cousin or not?" Drew demanded.

She won't have me!

Jack's mind shouted the words, even as his lips were clamped shut.

His memory played scenes from last night—Merritt working in the kitchen with Tillie, the two of them with heads bent over the counter workspace, whispering. Merritt's smile that had glanced off him when she'd looked up.

For the first time in decades, Jack wanted something more than his solitary existence.

But Merritt wasn't for him. She hadn't chosen him. He was playacting, trying to help her.

He was a fool for mollycoddling any emotions that felt real.

Drew scanned the ground that Jack had cleared. When he glanced up at Jack again, his eyes narrowed, like he didn't fully trust him.

Jack didn't trust himself.

Drew's hand dropped away from his shoulder at the same moment that Jack caught sight of movement, a body striding down the boardwalk. The gait was familiar . . .

Morris.

Recognition flashed through Jack in an instant. Morris had his head turned to the side, looking in a store window.

It was the chance Jack needed to turn his back.

"I gotta go," he told Drew.

The other man's brows started to pinch, but Jack couldn't stay here—not with Morris headed this way.

"Hang on—"

But Jack was already walking away. He cut through the corner of the site and ducked through the alley behind the café. Paused there. Morris should walk past the end of the street in three . . . two . . .

Jack hung back behind the edge of the building as Morris passed across the side street between two businesses and moved out of sight.

A beat of relief flowed, followed by a twist in Jack's gut.

Morris had been on that westbound train. Jack had

watched long enough while the train had chugged out of the station to know that the hired gun hadn't disembarked.

How had he ended up back in Calvin? He must've been on this morning's train. Must still be hunting Jack.

And Jack's first name was now known all around town, though he'd played fast and loose with the truth about his surname when Merritt had made assumptions.

Jack had never harbored hopes that somehow he'd end up with Merritt at the end of this. But if he had, this sighting of Morris would've been all he needed to set himself straight.

Jack had a past. One that might come looking for him at any moment.

And Morris wasn't even the worst of it. Merritt didn't know about his childhood, about how broken he really was.

Jack would never belong here.

And now he had to figure out a way to skirt Morris's notice while he helped Merritt finish the work for her pageant.

Guess he was going to see that preacher after all.

Merritt glanced up from where she was scratching ink onto a blank page at one of the tables in the dance hall, copying the pageant script onto one more piece of paper.

Jack was nearby, brushing blue paint onto one of the canvas-and-wood rectangle forms that made up the eight-foot-tall backdrop, a replacement for what had been lost.

Night was falling, and the circle of illumination thrown by the lamp she'd put on the table seemed to have shrunk.

Jack's lamp was burning low, and surely his stomach must be in want of supper.

She hadn't meant for him to get this education on what being married to a teacher was bound to be like for the months she'd finish out her contract—working long hours, preparing for the classroom.

Jack had shown up earlier after meeting with Mr. Carson, looking stymied, like one of her older students working a difficult arithmetic problem, and had surprised her by asking whether he could try his hand at painting. The children were gone now, after an abbreviated class time. They had been distracted by their surroundings, and without books, the memorization work was more tedious. For hours, she'd been aware of Jack as he'd worked on one of the large framed canvases stretched out on the floor, mostly sitting next to it but occasionally standing to move around the backdrop or wash out his paintbrush.

It had been his suggestion to keep working when, after the last child had left for the afternoon, she'd looked longingly at the stack of papers she needed to copy.

There was much work to be done and little time. Most of the children knew their lines, but one or two still needed to read from the paper.

Certain that her mind wouldn't stop its worrying, she put down the fountain pen and massaged her right hand in her lap. Jack looked over at the motion.

"Cramp?" he asked, placing his paintbrush in a mason jar of water nearby.

"Just tired muscles after a long day," she replied.

She stood, realizing how tight her muscles had become. The cavernous room had cooled as the evening had waned.

"You should've warned me it was getting dark," she muttered, touching the last page to test if the ink was dry before adding it to the stack of other scripts. "I'm sure you're completely bored after a long day observing my classroom."

He stood up, wiping his hands on a rag he pulled from his back pocket. "Not bored at all." When he glanced at her, she got a hint of the way he'd looked at her the night of the fire. Wanting, but hiding it. Or trying to.

"Drew said you were born to be a teacher," he said, throwing the words toward the floor as he stuffed away the rag and then bent to pick up the mason jar. "I can see what he meant. I think I would've boxed the ears of a couple of those boys, but you held your patience."

Pleasure flushed through her at the compliment.

"There are days where I do have to mete out punishment," she said. "Right now, we're all out of our element and discombobulated without a classroom to learn in."

She moved to gather her papers into a leather satchel.

"Did you always want to teach?" he asked quietly. He put the mason jar on the other side of the table and moved to the backdrop, grabbing one side of the heavy frame to lift it.

She hurried around the table to lift the other side, remembering the weight of the large wood pieces. He smiled his thanks.

"I wanted to be a writer," she said. "Or a painter. Something romantic." She laughed a little to hide the blush rising into her cheeks. "But my parents..." She trailed off, unsure whether she wanted to think about Maisey, about the past.

"Your parents didn't encourage it?"

Her smile had grown stiff as they dragged the frame to lean against the wall. "After ... " She couldn't bring herself to talk about Maisey after all. She swallowed back the sudden knot of tears that surprised her. "I was fifteen when my parents decided to move back east. My father grew up here. My mother was a transplant from Ohio. It was—things were too difficult for them to stay."

He rested the canvas and frame against the wall, dusting off his hands. She let go and hid her fisted hands in her skirt.

"I never wanted to be anywhere else," she said. She looked to the side but didn't see the wall that separated them from the outside. Only the vast prairie beyond, the Laramie Mountains in the distance, the sky that seemed to extend forever ...

"So I was given a choice," she finished. "Attend normal college and find a posting for a school, or move back east with my parents."

She'd walked back to the table, but he stood frozen where she'd left him. "That's an awful big decision for a fifteen-year-old. They couldn't stay long enough for you to finish schooling?"

She shook her head. It was easier to look at the two books she'd brought over from her house and lift them to her midsection than to look at him. "They really couldn't. It wasn't hard—"

"Liar," he said quietly. When had he come to stand beside her?

She lifted her chin slightly. "It isn't a lie."

A CONVENIENT BRIDE

"Sure it is." He was standing close enough to reach out and brush his thumb against the corner of her mouth. "When you tell an untruth, your mouth pulls. Just here."

His hand dropped away, and she felt the pulse of something just beneath her skin where he'd touched her.

She dipped her eyes. "Fine." Was she grinding her teeth? She couldn't seem to help it. "It was difficult, but only in the very beginning."

She remembered nights lying on a narrow cot in a girls' dormitory, silent tears streaming down her cheeks. Meals in a dining hall where everyone except her seemed to know each other.

"I did what seemed most natural and dove into my studies," she explained, her voice only a little uneven. "I loved the learning." That was true and she looked defiantly at him, daring him to challenge it. "And eventually I made friends." Including Darcy, who'd sent her a letter just today. Darcy's younger sister Elsie, who was like a little sister to Merritt, was in need of a teaching job. "Things got better. God provided this job for me, right in Calvin where I'd always wanted to be."

Jack was watching her face. His expression was more closed off now. She couldn't read him.

Books had always been easier. Perhaps she read too many romantic novels, but she'd rather thought he might reach out for her in this moment that seemed charged with . . . something.

And then he did reach out for her, his hand coming to cup her jaw.

Her pulse thrummed in her ears, her skin felt stretched

112

too tightly over her cheekbones. She felt alive and aware, and she tipped forward on her toes, her hand at her side moving to reach for him.

Only for him to swipe his thumb across her cheek and drop his hand away.

"You had a smudge of ink." His brows had creased, and he looked almost angry as he half turned away. He reached up to where a hat might rest on his head, huffed impatiently, and pushed his hand through his hair. "I miss my hat," he mumbled.

He'd turned away.

She'd thought he was pulling her close after the vulnerable confession, and he'd only been wiping away a smudge of ink.

Disappointment and humiliation warred as her cheeks flamed.

What had she been thinking? She clutched the books to her midsection, and her other hand trembled as she reached for the satchel.

"Here," he said. She didn't understand him until he reached for the books in her arms.

"I can get them," she said.

"I insist."

She didn't want him to insist. Not for this.

And she wasn't some fainting maiden from a silly romance novel. She smacked the books back onto the table. "I thought you were going to kiss me. You haven't kissed me once."

His eyes flared wide and he frowned, though she saw his throat work. "We shouldn't."

Shouldn't?

"Why not?"

He looked at her as if she were a hysterical female instead of one asking a simple question. "Because."

That wasn't an answer.

Before she could argue, he picked up the books and lifted the lampshade to blow out the wick. "We shouldn't be alone in here after dark. People might talk."

He was awfully worried about people talking, about her reputation.

It was endearing, in a way. Even if she didn't need protecting.

Her disappointment remained as she allowed him to escort her out of the dance hall. He glanced both ways down the boardwalk as they exited. Was he looking for someone?

But he'd closed himself off and she didn't dare ask him. Would he ever open up to her?

Eight

T HE MAN ACROSS THE TABLE FROM JACK made a little groan and flipped his cards onto the surface, face down.

A fold. Jack was the only one still betting, which meant he didn't have to reveal his cards. He pulled the small pile of coins from the center of the table and reached for the discarded cards and the deck so he could shuffle.

Movement behind the bar drew his eyes as his hands completed familiar motions.

It was the barkeep, a man who might be Jack's age, wiping down the bar.

Impatience flared, disappointment on its heels.

Jack had come to the saloon tonight to find out everything he could about Billy Burns. He'd settled in at the poker table, where men had come and gone as the night had worn on.

It was late now. He felt the pull of exhaustion as he dealt

the cards once more. Tonight wasn't about his winnings, though he was up over a dollar.

Burns had been helping his barman behind the long counter earlier in the night, when things had been busy. But he'd disappeared into an office behind the bar an hour ago and hadn't returned.

Jack needed to get out of town. He couldn't forget Morris was looking for him. But it was the pull toward Merritt that was becoming too much of a temptation.

He liked her. Too much.

All Jack needed was one or two vital facts about Burns. Some kind of leverage, a way to get him to back off on his plans to take the land. Jack wouldn't get the information he needed sitting out here with the handful of patrons left in the place at this late hour.

He folded without a word, tossing his cards face down on the table.

"Another hand?" The man with salt-and-pepper hair, sitting across from him, shuffled this time.

Jack flipped his ante to the center of the table.

He needed to finish this.

Merritt would be unhappy if she knew he was here. She didn't condone gambling. Or saloons.

He had almost kissed her today.

The memory had popped into his mind at inopportune times all night.

The softness of her skin beneath his fingertips. The flutter of her lashes, the way she'd leaned in . . .

The warmth of her breath, *right there* on his own lips.

He'd wanted it so badly.

Only his conscience shouting at him had prevented the kiss.

He forced away the memory of the hurt in her brown eyes and had to take a second look at his cards. The man across the table was almost asleep, but the one sitting kitty-corner to Jack wore a sharp look.

Merritt was a distraction, even in his memories.

Especially on the heels of meeting with Mr. Carson, the preacher. The man *hadn't* preached fire and brimstone after all. He'd read Jack a story about one man on a journey, who'd been beaten and robbed, and another man who'd come along and helped him. Jack didn't understand. And not understanding bothered him.

Where was Burns?

Jack's emotions were tangled in knots, and it was all because of Merritt.

She wasn't like anyone he'd ever met before. And when he was with her, he started to forget that he wasn't worthy.

Jack lost the next game and realized he'd missed a tell from the man at his side. Frustrated, he tried to tear his thoughts from the woman he couldn't seem to stop thinking about.

Voices rose from the staircase at the back of the room, tucked behind one edge of the bar. Jack's gaze flicked that direction.

"I'm not doing this!" A young woman in the skimpy dress he associated with a saloon girl was blocked in between the bar and the room by an older man who was beefy and had a gut hanging over the edge of his pants.

The man said something Jack couldn't make out. He reached for the girl's arm, but she jerked it away.

"I won't—"

The bartender moved that direction, having just served a pint to a man sitting at this end of the bar, and Jack felt some of the tension leave his shoulders. The barkeep would take care of it.

But instead of freeing the girl from the drunken patron, the bartender gestured toward the staircase. Jack only had a glimpse over the man's shoulder, but he saw the girl shake her head.

The drunken man said an expletive loud enough for Jack to hear. A glass mug was knocked off the back shelf and crashed to the ground, shattering.

The noise drew the attention of the other two men at Jack's table—but only for a second, and then they glanced back at their cards.

Didn't anyone else care that the girl might be in trouble?

"I said no!" she shouted now, struggling with the bartender, who had one of her arms in his grip.

The office door had come open about halfway. Jack sensed more than saw Burns's shadow listening behind the door.

Jack had laid low, stayed anonymous all evening while at the card table. Right now, he was just a face in the crowd.

If he intervened in the scuffle, he'd be visible. The barkeep would associate his face with this moment. Wouldn't share information he otherwise might. Jack would lose his chance at digging up leverage on Burns, lose his chance to help Merritt keep the school land.

But the woman was crying now, a wobble in her voice as she said, "Stop!"

And Jack heard a memory-echo of his thirteen-year-old voice saying the very same thing. *Stop! Don't hurt him!*

He was out of his chair, his winnings quickly scooped up and stuffed into his pocket, before he could think.

"'Scuse me!" He strode across the room, hailing the bartender, who turned toward him, still behind the bar.

Jack had a clear view of the lecherous, drunken man with one arm clasped around the young woman, holding her against his side. She was struggling against him, but she was slight and obviously didn't know how to fight someone so large.

"Why don't you leave her alone?" Jack asked. "She don't seem to want your company."

"I paid for hers," the man growled. "Stay out of it."

Hand still in his pocket, Jack closed his fist around the coins he'd just put there. "I'll refund your money." Quick as a rattlesnake strike, he ripped his hand out of his pocket and flung the coins at the man. Two struck him in the face, and he cried out, his hold on the girl loosening.

It was the opening Jack needed. He landed a right-handed jab on the man's nose, heard a satisfying crunch.

The bartender shouted something, but Jack wasn't waiting around for the man to jump over the bar.

Jack grabbed the girl's wrist and tugged her away from the paunchy man, pulling her toward the exit.

She was right on his heels.

He threw a look over his shoulder in time to see Burns

in the doorway of his office, eyes narrowed on Jack as he made the exit.

Jack went out into the darkness, still clutching the girl's wrist.

He'd been seen. He'd known it would happen but still felt the beat of disappointment.

The girl immediately started shivering in the night air, and he shucked his coat to wrap it around her shoulders.

He could hear raised voices through the swinging doors.

"We can't stay here," he told her. He was already moving down the boardwalk, and she followed him, though hesitantly. The one clear thought in his mind was, *Merritt . . . bring her to Merritt's.*

"Who are you?" There was still the hiccup of a sob in her voice, a wariness he was thankful for. She'd gotten herself into trouble in that saloon and wasn't sure she was out of it yet. "Why'd you help me?"

"Because it was the right thing to do." Even though it'd ruined his chances of easily digging up dirt on Burns. "I'm Jack. A friend of Merritt Harding."

At his words, a bit of tension seeped out of her. She knew Merritt, if only by reputation. A cold wind bit through Jack's shirt as he urged her to hurry past the next alleyway and keep walking down the boardwalk.

"You got somewhere to go?" he asked. "Maybe some family you can stay with?" She wouldn't be able to go back to the bar now.

Her sniffles turned into full-blown sobs. "I've got a room—a rented room—but I'm getting thrown out. I was working at the café until the fire, and I—I—"

She was so worked up she could barely speak.

"It's all right," he told her. "I'm taking you somewhere safe."

His adrenaline was fading now, leaving him exhausted. But the clarity that had hit him as they'd run out of the saloon hadn't faded.

His one thought in that moment had been to go to Merritt. That's where he wanted to be.

But the girl—he realized he didn't even know her name—turned worried eyes on him. "I have to go get him—my son."

Merritt was rousted from bed at the pounding on her door.

She'd been up late, copying more scripts, and it felt as if she'd barely slept at all. She was confused, discombobulated as she pushed up on her elbow. The room was dark around her. Dawn hadn't broken yet. What time was it?

Had she dreamed the knock?

But it came again, *thud, thud, thud* on her front door.

And Jack's voice, muffled and muted through the two doors between them, "Merritt, I need you."

Jack!

Her sluggish thoughts cleared as she got out of bed, shivering when her bare feet hit the plank floor. She grabbed her wrapper from the foot of the bed and then thought better of it.

If Jack was outside at this hour, she'd better get dressed. She pulled on her dress and frantically buttoned it.

"I'm coming!" she called out before he could barrage the door again. What if her neighbors heard? What was he thinking?

Was he in trouble?

She imagined she heard a baby's cry. What in the world was going on?

She was overly aware of her bare feet and the fact that her hair must be in disarray as she rushed to the front door and opened it.

Jack was there, but standing back from the door as if he was concerned he might scare her. His face was in shadow.

"What—"

There was movement behind him. A shuffling of feet. And Merritt realized there was a young woman standing in his shadow. She was holding a baby wrapped in a blanket.

"Come inside." Merritt opened the door and scooted backward into the room as the chill from outside wafted over her bare feet. "What's the matter? What's happened?"

She reached for a lamp on the side table and scrambled to light the wick. When the small flame lit the room, she turned back and saw Jack settling the young mother on a sofa.

He was in his shirtsleeves, and he was shivering. She saw it even though he tried to mask the motion.

She realized the young woman was wearing his coat.

"I'll put on some coffee," she said. "Jack, come with me."

"I'll be back in a minute," he told the young woman.

His tread on the floor was so much louder than the quiet shuffle of her bare feet, and she was aware of her barely dressed state and that it was the middle of the night—or was it coming on to morning?

She squinted out the kitchen window and saw the tiniest slice of silver light on the horizon. It was morning, but the late hour she'd gone to bed made it feel like she hadn't slept at all.

She moved to the stove, quickly bending to stir the coals and tuck kindling inside.

Jack stood at a respectful distance, but before she closed the door and plunged them into shadow again, she saw the red chapped skin of his hands.

"What is going on?" she demanded in a whisper.

Last night, she'd left her shawl lying over the back of one of the kitchen chairs, and she went to grab it. He stood still while she crossed the room back toward him, even as she tossed the knitted shawl around his shoulders.

It was dark and she was close, and she couldn't tell whether the twitch of his lips was bemusement or something else. He did look a little silly, but she noticed the way he tucked his hands under his arms, crossed across his chest.

"She was in trouble," he started. "The only place I could think to come was here."

There was something in his voice when he said the words. Consternation maybe, or another emotion she couldn't place.

It would help if she could see his face. She went to the shelf and pulled down another lamp.

"You'd better start at the beginning."

He sighed. "I was playing a hand of poker at the saloon."

She lost her hold on the lamp, and it thunked onto the

table. "What in the world were you doing there?" She couldn't quite contain the sharpness in her tone. He was silent as she struck a match and lit the lamp.

When she turned to face him, he'd shut himself away again. She could see it in his expression. The openness from only moments ago was gone.

But then he exhaled a frustrated sigh and pushed both hands through his hair, nearly dislodging the shawl. "I will tell you everything." He didn't sound happy about that, his voice low and almost angry. "But for now, let me explain about Miss Bauer."

By the time he told her about the near-fight at the saloon, her heart was thrumming in her throat.

He could've been killed. She'd heard Danna talk plenty of times about how men who'd been drinking were quick to pull out a knife or gun.

Merritt didn't know whether to be angry or grateful that he'd helped Velora Bauer.

"She's new in town," he said. "Her husband passed just before the baby was born. She'd been working at the café before it closed for repairs."

He glanced into the sitting room, where the baby had begun crying again. "You got any porridge or . . . eggs, maybe? I think he's hungry. She probably is too."

Merritt moved to the basket of fresh eggs on the counter even as her mind clicked through all the information Jack had divulged.

"The lady she's renting from is throwing her out. She had nowhere to go with the baby and thought—"

Merritt could guess what she'd thought. The young

woman had been desperate to provide for her child. Thank God Velora hadn't been able to go through with it.

She sighed. "Of course I'll help, and I'm glad you were there."

Something sparked in his eyes.

The baby's cries grew louder, and he tipped his head toward the sitting room. "I'm gonna see if I can help."

Merritt's fork scraped the pan as she stirred the scrambled eggs. She had a little savings put away. Less now that she'd spent some money trying to resupply the classroom. How else might she help the young widow?

For one wild moment, she pictured sending the young woman to her cousins. The McGraw brothers desperately needed a woman's touch at the ranch. Tillie and Jo were running wild, and David hadn't had as much schooling as he needed. Drew hadn't been the same since Amanda had left him. The men were a little rough around the edges, but they were good stock.

But she knew Drew would kill her if she made the suggestion.

She'd enlist the help of her friend Penny's mother. Mrs. Castlerock's husband was a wealthy banker known for his stingy ways, but the older couple had plenty of room in their mansion and could possibly spare some funds to get Velora on her feet again.

The eggs done, she realized the baby had quieted. She put the eggs on a plate and crept to the doorway.

Jack stood at the window, staring outside with the baby at his shoulder. He was patting the babe's back while the one-year-old chewed on his fist.

Velora had fallen asleep on the sofa, one arm tucked beneath her head.

There was something about seeing the man holding a baby that twisted Merritt's insides in a way that was both pleasurable and painful. Jack was a natural with children. She'd seen it in the classroom.

She turned back to the kitchen, not so dark now with the sun coming over the horizon.

Jack might be good with children, but he'd been keeping secrets from her.

Did she want to live with a man she couldn't entirely trust? It felt so easy to succumb to his charm.

But if she married him, would she regret it?

An hour later, both baby and Velora had eaten and retired to Merritt's bedroom to rest with the door closed. Merritt would take them to visit Mrs. Castlerock later and see what could be done.

And Merritt was left with Jack in the sitting room. He'd moved to sit on a sofa and had his elbows on his knees with his head in his hands as she entered the room.

He looked up, dropped his hands as she set a mug of coffee in front of him on the low table.

He looked tired. Or haunted.

She stood against the bookcase, her hands behind her back. "Talk to me," she said.

Her stomach was twisted in knots. This moment felt fraught with tension, like she was standing on the edge of a cliff. One step, one shift, could change everything.

He sighed but held her gaze. "On my first night here—I suppose it was the second, after the night of the fire—I overheard a couple of men talking. About the school. About you."

She couldn't help but notice that he didn't say *where* he'd overheard the men.

But that detail was quickly forgotten as he explained what he'd heard and what he'd discovered since. That he'd enlisted Drew's help.

"Is that why you've been spending all your spare moments cleaning up the building site?"

He seemed surprised that she knew about that. Small-town gossip spread like wildfire.

"I can handle Mr. Polk," she told Jack, though it hurt to think about being replaced in the classroom before she was ready. She would think about that later. "You told Drew. Why didn't you tell me?"

He stood from the sofa, moving across the room toward the kitchen and then spinning back to face her. "I was trying to protect you, I guess." His hand had come up to rub the back of his neck.

He wanted to protect her. Even though she couldn't agree with keeping secrets or how he'd gone about parts of it, the thought warmed her.

This was the moment. The cliff's edge.

"There's a lot we're still discovering about each other," she said, "but I'm coming to know you."

He looked almost battered by her words.

Spurred on by the strength of her emotions, she took a step toward him. And another.

"I want to marry you." She hadn't said it quite like that since they'd met. Everything had been planned, and she'd kept following the plan, even through her misgivings. But the words she'd said were the truth. She wanted to be with the Jack who cuddled babies and protected her.

Another step toward him. "I don't want secrets between us. I want a life with you—"

She'd come close enough to see the dark flecks in his color-shifting eyes. Hazel this morning and clouded with . . . hope?

Merritt had been planning to reach for him, but it was Jack whose hands spanned her waist first.

His head dipped and he groaned just before his lips crashed against hers. There was no finesse, simply a desperation behind the kiss that made her breathless. The feeling that he couldn't bear *not* to be kissing her.

Her hands came up to fist in the shoulders of his shirt.

He broke the kiss for a fractured moment, his breath warm on her lips and chin.

His eyes were stormy.

And then his hand came up to cup her jaw gently, and this time when he pressed his lips to hers, there was a reverence to it. It felt like a new beginning.

Like everything she wanted.

A tiny cry from the baby, the sound of a tread from the bedroom, and the door snicking open had Jack brushing a kiss at the spot where her nose met her forehead, then releasing her to take a step back.

The stormy look had cleared from his eyes, and she couldn't read them now.

MERRITT SMOOTHED THE SKIRT OF the sky-blue dress, twisting in front of the kitchen window to try and see her head-to-toe reflection in the wavy glass. Night had fallen, but the lamp on the table didn't throw enough illumination to show her reflection clearly, even though it was dark outside.

She'd been a young girl the last time she'd had a store-bought dress. Mostly, she sewed her own. The fancy stitching and hint of lace at her wrists made this gown special.

She was going to marry Jack in two days. This was to be her wedding dress.

She pressed the fingers of one hand against her mouth in realization. In thirty-six hours, she'd belong to Jack. They'd be a family. She'd have a husband of her own. A family, more than the snatches of hours she got to spend with her cousins every few weeks. She wasn't going to be alone anymore.

She twirled in the middle of the room, idly watching her reflection. Imagined Jack dancing with her, one strong hand at her waist. Holding her like he had just this morning.

After settling Velora and the baby with Mrs. Castlerock, who'd promised to get the church ladies involved in their care, Merritt had spent her morning in the makeshift classroom, teaching her last lesson of the calendar year. Tomorrow, they'd spend their classroom hours in final preparations for the pageant on Monday.

She'd been in the middle of coaching Samuel through an arithmetic problem, leaning over his shoulder and pointing at his slate, when Mr. Polk had come into the dance hall. He hadn't said a word to her but had spent over an hour observing. A silent figure, towering at the back of the room.

Before today, his presence would've made her nervous, made her overthink every action, every word she said to the children.

After what Jack had divulged, she'd only been angry at Mr. Polk's interference. She'd stuffed the emotion away, concentrating on the children and what they needed. Her job might be threatened, but she'd fight for it.

The perfect idea for how to make that happen had come to her during a quiet supper alone, and she had spent the rest of the evening making plans. What could be better than an auction benefiting their school? And right before Christmas, when folks might feel more generous or need to buy a last-minute gift. The papers she'd scribbled notes on were spread across the table.

But once her steam had run out, she'd started thinking

about the wedding. And this dress. When she'd seen Danna in passing earlier this week, she'd asked her friend to stop by and see it. She could always count on Danna to tell her the truth. Danna was a straight shooter, a no-nonsense kind of person.

If the dress was too much or made Merritt's skin look sickly, Danna would tell her.

A soft knock sounded at the door. That must be Danna now.

Merritt's skirts rustled around her as she moved through the sitting room, where she'd lit a lamp in expectation of her friend's arrival, and opened the door.

It wasn't Danna on the other side. Her heart leaped as she registered Jack. He was facing away, staring pointedly into the darkness.

He only flicked one quick glance at her before backing toward the door. "Can I come in?"

Merritt's heart was pounding. He wasn't supposed to see her dress before the wedding! And she also wrestled a sinking feeling of disappointment as she backed into the room to allow him inside. He had to have seen the dress, but there'd been no reaction.

Maybe it wasn't as special as she'd thought.

He shut the door with a decisive click and turned to face her, hands on his hips beneath his coat.

He blinked. His eyes raked up and down, and his hands dropped to his sides.

The disappointment she'd felt seconds ago swelled and changed into something else entirely at the look in his eyes.

"What—" He cleared his throat, and his eyes jumped to her face. "You look—I can't—" He shook his head.

A sense of shyness threatened to overtake her, but she fought through it, just as she fought off the blush stealing up into her neck.

"I've never rendered someone speechless before. I suppose the dress was a good investment."

If Jack kept looking at her like that, she'd wear the dress every Sunday to church. Maybe Saturdays too.

"It's not the dress." There was a roughness to his voice that sent prickles of goosebumps up her arms. "It's you. You're beautiful. Like a princess from some book."

Pleasure suffused her. She'd been trying not to think about the kiss Jack had given her this morning, but it had broken into her thoughts in quiet moments throughout the day.

He stuffed his hands in his pockets, still looking at her with warmth in his eyes, and scooted around her toward the kitchen. "You mind if I make a pot of coffee?"

She followed a step behind him, stopping in the doorway when he crossed toward the stove and the shelf where she kept her coffeepot.

He filled the pot with water but hesitated before bringing it to the stove.

"I'm happy for you to make yourself at home," she murmured, leaning one hip against the doorway. "This will be your home, too, in another two days."

He'd turned away from her to put the pot on, but she saw the way one hand fisted at his side.

"I need to—"

"I'm disappointed—"

Their words tumbled over each other and he half smiled. "What're you disappointed about?"

She jutted her chin up. "I thought you might kiss me hello. Didn't you want to?"

If he was upset by her directness, he didn't show it. "The wanting is the problem," he said dryly. "If I let myself get too close, I won't want to let you go."

Oh.

Warmth crept into her neck.

There was a sincerity that rang through his words, something in his tone that she couldn't understand.

"You won't have to let me go, not after Sunday."

He moved to the shelf to pull down two tin mugs. The scent of coffee began to filter through the room. "I know you've got your plans. I was talking to Mr. Carson today after our meeting and started thinking . . . you and I don't have to rush things."

Her stomach swooped. Rush things? Didn't he want to marry her? Confusion swirled. Hadn't he just said he didn't want to let her go?

"I've been thinking . . . won't you want your parents to be here to see you married? We could send them train tickets . . . "

He'd spoken the words over his shoulder but trailed off as he turned to face her, still across the room.

"They won't return to Calvin," she said quietly. Was this why he'd wanted to delay the wedding? Thinking of her parents?

"Why not. You're their only daughter, aren't you?"

She exhaled a long breath through her nose. "I am— now."

She saw his confusion in the wrinkle of his brow.

She moved toward the table and sat down, careful not to wrinkle her skirts. "I suppose if I'm asking for there to be no secrets between us, you deserve to know."

He took the pot off the stove and moved to the counter to pour. "I'm listening."

She moved the papers into a stack, nervously flicking through their edges. "I had an older sister, Maisey. She was twelve when she died. She'd gone swimming in a little water hole, a pond in someone's property, and there—" Merritt's voice broke.

Jack moved close, setting her coffee cup on the table in front of her. He touched the back of her shoulder blade with his warm palm, and it gave her the strength to go on.

"There was a terrible accident, and she drowned." Saying the words quickly was the only way she could get them out.

He sat down in the chair next to her, his knee pressing into her skirts. His hand closed over hers in her lap. It was only with his warmth surrounding her that she realized how cold her own skin had grown.

"My parents drowned too, in a way. They disappeared into their grief. My mother couldn't bear to eat. My father spent hours alone in the barn."

Merritt had been left to her own devices—a younger sister who had missed Maisey with a fierce grief that she hadn't known how to process.

A tear slipped down her cheek, and she whisked it away before it could fall on the skirt of her dress. Tried to smile a wobbly smile. "It's silly, I know. I remember my next birth-day, after . . . after . . . " She couldn't say the words again. "I woke feeling both excited and sad. I missed her greatly, but it was also my birthday. A day to be celebrated. But my mother couldn't pull herself out of bed. And my father was nowhere to be found."

There'd been no cake. No gifts.

Merritt had felt guilty for expecting anything at all. And forgotten, like she was only a shadow. The sister who'd lived but who didn't really exist anymore.

She tipped her chin up, staying more tears by sheer strength of will. "I found solace in books," she said. "Maisey had taught me to read. And I could slip into the pages of a book and be someone else for a while. Someone brave. Someone adventurous." Someone wanted.

She had lost herself in books and in her studies for a long time.

"That's why they left town, left you to become a teacher without any support."

Jack said the words in an even tone, but she heard the underlying anger.

She finally gained the courage to look at him. His eyes were full of concern.

"It's all right," she told him. "I have my cousins, and friends in town. And you. I don't mind that my parents can't return for the wedding."

Thinking about the wedding made her remember the round box sitting half hidden behind a sofa in the sitting room.

"I've got something for you," she told him. "Hold on."

She rose from the table and went to fetch it. The box filled her arms, and she could feel her heart drumming in her chest as nerves overcame her.

"I was going to save it for a wedding and Christmas gift, but I think you should open it now."

He was sitting in the chair where she'd left him, turned away from the table, and he stared at her, perplexed. "A gift? For me?"

Jack didn't know what to say as Merritt pressed what looked to be a hat box into his hands.

He turned it around, uncertain.

"Open it," she prompted.

He could barely look at her in that dress. He'd walked inside, still raw and reeling from the kiss they'd shared that morning. Still fighting with himself, Mr. Carson's story from earlier today echoing in the back of his mind. The story of a boy who'd taken his inheritance and walked out on his family. Who'd lost everything and come crawling back.

Jack could relate to the boy in the story, except Jack had no one to come crawling back to . . .

Merritt.

There'd been a moment this morning, while she was talking, when his selfish nature had roared to life, and he'd known—this woman, this life. She was what he wanted.

Ever since he'd arrived in town, he'd told himself she wasn't for him. But he was so tired of fighting—

And he'd given in. Taken the kiss he shouldn't have.

Taken the adoring way she'd looked at him when he'd drawn back.

He'd been fighting with himself all day, trying to figure out if there was a way he could stay in Calvin, build a life with Merritt.

He didn't know any way of supporting himself other than gambling. He'd spent his teenage years working on the Farrs' farm, but he didn't know how to manage one.

And there was the matter of Morris, and Jack's past catching up to him.

He'd come here tonight to ask if she'd be willing to wait. Wait until he figured some things out. He'd brought up her parents to see whether that might buy him some time.

He hadn't expected what she'd shared.

"Come on," she said with a little laugh. She was still standing nearby, watching him expectantly. "It's a gift, not a rattlesnake."

He kept his eyes on the box he held in his hands. "I've never been given a Christmas gift before."

He slipped the lid open as he said the words, and found a dark-brown wool cowboy hat inside. Nearly the same as the one he'd lost, only brand-new.

He had to clear his throat of emotion before he could speak. "It's a fine hat."

His hand trembled slightly as he took it out of the box.

She was looking at him with shadowed eyes. "How is it possible you've never received a Christmas gift before?"

He stood, overwhelmed with emotion he shouldn't be feeling, and tipped the hat onto his head. Turned away, because it was too difficult to look at her in this moment.

I don't want secrets between us.

Her words from this morning echoed in his mind, and everything he was keeping bottled up boiled inside him, like a pot with the lid ready to blow off.

She'd figure it out if he stayed, if he married her. Merritt was smart.

"I'm not the man who wrote those letters." The words tasted like ash in his mouth. This was the moment she'd tell him to get out, to leave and never come back. The pain of it tore through his gut.

But when he turned to her, she was looking at the hat, and then her gaze trickled down to the rest of him.

"I've already pieced together some of it," she said softly, no judgment in her eyes. "You wrote certain things, trying to present yourself in the best light."

I'm not John!

She didn't get it, and the words to tell her so were right there on his lips.

But he chickened out. Told her a different truth instead, delaying the moment when he'd reveal his identity.

"I never knew my parents."

He couldn't watch her, quailed under the compassion in her gaze and turned to look out the darkened window. Blinked at the reflection of himself in that hat.

"My first memories are of sleeping in a dormitory in a Chicago orphanage. Eating meals that never quite filled me up at a table so long and so filled with kids just like me that I never could see the end of it."

Those were the good memories.

He gripped the counter with both hands as he forced

himself to say the rest of it. "When I was eleven, I was shipped west on a train, along with a car full of other orphaned children."

He heard her soft intake of air and the rustle of her skirts, felt motion behind him as she sidled closer.

"The caretaker at our orphanage said we'd find families, but we were all pretty scared."

He'd met Dewey on the train that day. The boy had been from another orphanage, and Jack had hardly known anyone at all. Dewey, three years younger, had been hiding his tears behind angry words, and Jack had known he'd have to calm the boy down or all of them would be in a heap of trouble.

So he'd started spinning yarns. Stories about the homes they'd find. Stories about a hero detective who helped people in the city they'd just left. Stories that he'd almost started to believe in himself. How could he not when the kids around him watched and listened with wide-eyed attention, believing that he was a hero himself, just because he told the stories?

"It took a while before I got taken in by a family. Me and Dewey."

Jack had been disillusioned by then, watching the younger children, the delicate girls, be adopted. Dewey too, though he'd stuck by Jack's side and still pretended to believe it when Jack told the story of the family they'd find together.

"They only wanted me. The—Farrs." He was unable to hide the roughness of his voice. "But I talked fast"—the way he always had—"and convinced them to take Dewey and me both." Jack had insisted they were brothers—the new scar on his palm had seemed so important.

What had happened later had been his fault. It was so clear now.

"They didn't want a pair of sons," he said. "They wanted hands to work their farm. Mrs. Farr was . . . " He bit back the sudden cry that wanted to emerge. Merritt was so quiet he couldn't even hear her breathing. "If she'd been consistent in her anger, it would've been one thing. But a simple mistake made one day would get a scolding. A similar mistake the next might earn a beating."

He'd never known what might set her off. He'd tried to guess, tried to complete every chore, keep the farm clean.

Jack coughed to cover the sob that wanted to escape. "She gave Dewey such a bad beating that he never recovered."

Stop!

Jack had tried to stop her. He'd been fourteen and almost as tall as Mrs. Farr, but she'd had a thick leather belt in hand and had turned it on him while Dewey lay bleeding on the floor.

"He died a few weeks later." Dewey hadn't been right, even after a few days had passed. Had complained of stomach pains and headaches as he'd lain in his cot in the lean-to that was supposed to be their bedroom. Jack had covered for him, doing all his own chores along with all of Dewey's. Jack'd been trying to devise a plan for the two of them to run away, but then it was too late.

It wasn't right. It wasn't fair, what'd happened to Dewey. Jack had been young, helpless to do anything about the injustice his brother had suffered at the hands of Mrs. Farr. When he'd run away, he'd promised himself he'd never let something like that happen again.

Merritt's arms came around him from behind. She pressed herself against him, pressed her face into the back of his shoulder. "I'm sorry," she murmured. "I'm so sorry. It wasn't right. You shouldn't have had to live through that."

It was my fault.

He couldn't say the words out loud, though they lived inside him.

If he hadn't begged for his "brother" to come and live with the Farrs, Dewey would still be alive. If he'd fought harder . . . if he'd convinced his brother to run away . . .

Merritt held him for long moments, long enough for him to regain his composure.

I'm not John.

She loosened her grip on him, and he turned to face her, to say the words, but he didn't get the chance.

She pressed both palms to his cheeks, reached up on tiptoe, and pressed her lips to his in a seeking kiss.

He felt it all. Her care, her sadness—maybe for herself, maybe for the boy he'd been.

He drank her in like a man dying of thirst.

When she pulled back, he saw the tears tracking down her cheeks. He reached up to sweep them away with his thumb, saw more sparkling in her eyes.

She was compassionate and fiery and everything he hadn't known he wanted—

A sharp knock on the door startled him into stepping

back. He bumped into the counter. Felt for the hat that had been knocked askew.

Merritt glanced over her shoulder. "That'll be Danna. We planned to get together."

He nodded, trying to rein in emotions he hadn't let loose in ages. What was he doing?

Merritt swept both hands across her cheeks, clearing away the evidence of her tears.

He followed her into the front room. He felt raw and exposed. And the last thing he wanted was for the town marshal to find out his identity.

When Danna stepped inside wearing her trousers and vest, a baby in the crook of one arm, he was confounded for the briefest moment. The marshal was a mother? He reached up to tip his hat. Her sharp eyes took it in.

"I'll take my leave," he told the both of them. "See you tomorrow." Those words were for Merritt, and when he looked at her, he felt a beat of the invisible connection they shared. Somehow, talking about his past had bonded them. He'd expected the opposite—for the knowledge to drive her away.

"I'll step outside with you." The marshal's easy words put his hackles up.

The door closed behind them. She rocked slightly where she stood on the step.

Jack didn't want to talk to her, but he couldn't walk away when she'd so obviously followed him outside.

In the dark, he couldn't read her expression.

"Word around town is there's someone looking for you. Or rather, for Jack Easton. That's not you . . . is it?"

Morris.

He didn't say anything. Merritt was the one who'd asked for no more secrets.

But somehow it didn't sit right to lie to the marshal. Maybe because she was Merritt's friend. Or maybe he was having some strange attack of conscience.

She sighed, almost silent in the darkness.

"I can help you," she said quietly. "But you've got to let me know how."

"Is that all?" he drawled. "Merritt's been waiting on you."

He didn't say goodbye as she slipped back inside the house.

It wasn't Danna's job to look out for Morris. Jack hadn't been able to tell Merritt the rest of it—that he wasn't John at all. That this had been a farce from the beginning.

If he truly wanted to stay, he had to make things right himself.

Ten

C OME IN, COME IN."
Mrs. Ewing held open the door to her small apartment above the milliner's store and ushered Merritt and Jack inside. The seamstress had lived here for as long as Merritt had known her, while the milliner lived in one of the houses on Merritt's street.

It was almost dark and the wind had changed directions late in the afternoon, coming straight out of the north with an icy bite.

"Thank you for having us," Merritt said as she was enveloped by the warmth from the stove in one corner of the room. She loosened her scarf, aware of Jack unbuttoning his coat behind her.

"Would you like some coffee?" Mrs. Ewing asked. "Clarissa made some cinnamon cookies yesterday."

Jack hung back near the door.

I'm not fit for company.

He'd said the words with a self-deprecating smile when she'd met him at the school site and asked him to accompany her. She knew he'd been out at the site most of the day, cleaning away the rubble. He'd stomped ash off his boots to prove his point.

But she'd cajoled until he'd given in.

And when he would've stayed near the door, she slipped her hand into his and tugged him over to the sofa to sit beside her.

Mrs. Ewing bustled into the kitchenette, rattling a plate with her back turned to them.

You're wanted.

Merritt willed the words to reach Jack, though she didn't dare speak them aloud. She'd dreamed about him last night, the little boy he must've been. On his own. No family except the one he'd forged. No one to rescue him when he'd needed it.

It was incredible that he'd grown up to be a man of honor despite his beginnings. Oh, perhaps he had a propensity to keep secrets, but didn't he have reason? For so long, he'd had no one to confide in.

She could be the person he confided in.

Her reasons for wanting to marry had been self-centered. She'd wanted a family of her own.

But now she wanted to give Jack a family. To show him the unconditional love she'd received before Maisey had died.

That's why her hand curled around his where they sat on the sofa.

She caught his sideways glance as Mrs. Ewing crossed

the room, a china plate in each hand. Merritt had to let go of Jack to take the treat offered to her. She murmured her thanks.

"It's you who should be thanked," Mrs. Ewing said. "Clarissa has been talking of nothing else but the pageant for weeks. You've made her Christmas by figurin' out a place to hold it after all that's happened."

Merritt let the pleasure of the compliment wash over her. Jack bit into his cookie and expressed his delight, which made the woman straighten her shoulders with pride.

"Let me show you my donation," Mrs. Ewing said as she bustled toward the bedroom door.

Merritt heard the rumble of Jack's stomach. She had plans for later in the evening and hadn't thought to plan for supper.

"Did you eat lunch?" she whispered to him.

At his shrug, she slipped him the second half of her cookie and caught the flash of warmth in his eyes just before Mrs. Ewing came back out of the room with a dove-gray dress over one arm.

Merritt balanced her plate on the sofa beside Jack and stood up to go to the woman.

"It's lovely!" she exclaimed. "Look at the lacework, Jack."

Mrs. Ewing beamed with pride as she held up one of the sleeves for Jack to see, careful to keep the hem of the dress off the ground.

"Pretty." But when Merritt looked back at him, his gaze was on her.

She flushed.

There was a matching heat in his gaze before his eyes cut away.

Within minutes, Mrs. Ewing had wrapped the dress in crisp brown paper, and Merritt and Jack were sent on their way after a flurry of thank-yous.

"Want me to hold your package?" Jack asked as they descended the last stairs onto the boardwalk. The milliner's shop was on the opposite end of town from Merritt's home, but she set a brisk pace, face turned into her scarf.

"I've got it." The dress wasn't heavy, just awkward and bulky. Mrs. Ewing hadn't wanted to wrinkle the fine fabric and had only folded it once, making it a large parcel.

"Where to?" he asked her.

"Home."

She felt rather than heard the quick inhale of breath that he seemed to hold.

Home.

Had Jack ever had one before?

"I'm sorry we can't spend the evening together," she murmured. "But there is always tomorrow. And the day after that. And the day after . . . "

Tomorrow morning, in the preacher's parlor before the worship service, she would become Mrs. Jack Crosby. Anticipation swirled in her belly, the way it had every time the very same thought had caught her off guard today.

Jack was quiet as their boots thudded on the boardwalk, taking them past a darkened storefront. Another block, past the Happy Cowboy saloon, and they'd turn down her street.

"Will you have enough donations for the auction?" he asked.

"This dress will fetch a pretty penny," she said, hugging the dear package to her middle, though careful not to crinkle the paper. "And the Castlerocks have promised to match the total of all our donations."

She suspected it was the handiwork of her friend Penny's mother. Despite being notoriously stingy, Mr. Castlerock had a soft spot for his wife and daughter. But it didn't matter who'd made the pledge, only that it had been made. Merritt's living room was filled with donation items, like the fancy mantel clock donated by the mercantile store, a batch of ten gift certificates for supper at the café—once it was back up and running—and a fine leather saddle from the new leatherworks in town.

Everyone Merritt had spoken to had thought having an auction just before the pageant was a brilliant idea. But she never would've come up with the idea if it hadn't been for Jack and his urgency to get the school rebuilt.

Everything was going according to plan.

As they walked past a square of light cast on the ground through the saloon's window, the doors swung open and several bodies pressed outside.

Jack began to speak. "I need to tell you—"

There was an incomprehensible shout, and Merritt found herself flung completely off the boardwalk, fumbling for balance and not finding it.

She lost hold of the package, her arms flying out in front of her as the ground rushed up to meet her.

She hit hard, her knees and hands taking the brunt of the fall. She fought to catch her breath.

A raucous laugh broke out, quickly quieting as footsteps faded away into the night.

"Merritt!" Jack must've jumped off the boardwalk, because she heard the clomp of both his feet hitting the dirt lane.

"Don't step on the dress—" She scrabbled to find it in the dark, her palms burning. How far had she flung it away as she'd tried to catch herself?

"Never mind about the dress." His hands came to her shoulders and then her waist, lifting her to her feet.

He stayed close, his hands roaming her arms as if to check for injury. Was he watching over her shoulder, where the men had gone?

"Are you hurt?"

"I don't think so. My knees are scraped, but I'm all right."

He made a harsh sound in the darkness and she shivered.

"Let's get you home."

She'd never heard his voice so commanding.

"Jack, the dress!" she exclaimed when he banded his arm around her waist and would've led her away without it.

He made an angry noise and went back, carefully scooping up the package. He curled his arm about her shoulders and ushered her along the street to where they would've come off the boardwalk anyway.

He was quiet and seemed to be seething as they passed the two blocks until they reached her bungalow.

Light illuminated the lane from inside the house. In the last few moments, she'd forgotten about her company.

"Danna and my good friend Corrine are here, along with a few others."

The door opened and feminine voices emerged.

Jack held back as a woman who could only be Corrine came outside in a flurry of skirts and lace.

"She took a tumble off the boardwalk," he said quickly. "Coupla drunk men shoved right into her. Can you check her over?"

Merritt laughed a little. "I'm fine. I told you, my knees might be scraped." A pulse of pain there echoed her words.

Corrine was making sympathetic noises, but Merritt pushed the wrapped dress into her friend's hands.

"Jack!" He'd already moved a couple of steps away, but he turned back in the darkness.

She went to him, pressed in close and wound her arms around his waist.

"I'll miss you tonight."

He was curiously still. She'd thought his arms would come around her, but maybe he was conscious of Corrine still behind her.

"I'll see you at the church in the morning," she said softly.

She reached up on tiptoe, but her lips met the cool skin of his cheek.

"Goodbye."

There was a finality to his words as he slipped away into the darkness.

She let the warmth of her friends' chatter slip over her, their exclamations over her skinned palms, but her heart followed Jack into the night.

Jack only walked as far as Merritt's neighbor's house, then doubled back in the small alleyway behind the row of tidy houses.

He stood outside at the back corner of Merritt's house, in a patch of darkness between two windows. A place where her marshal friend wouldn't be able to look outside and see him if he happened to move.

He felt breathless with fear, adrenaline still pumping after the near-miss on the boardwalk outside that saloon.

He hadn't seen who'd given Merritt the push, but in the fractured second before he'd been able to react, he'd seen the flash of a face in the light thrown by the saloon door that had closed an instant later.

Morris.

Her fall had been no accident, Jack was sure of that.

He couldn't figure out why. Had Morris been trailing them? Jack had spent all afternoon out in the open at the school site, praying that Morris would seek him out. Hoping that the man could be talked down from whatever violence he wanted to do to get that money back.

Was it possible the man had followed him and Merritt down to the milliner's, then back again? It seemed too coincidental that he'd come out of the saloon at just the right moment to knock into Merritt.

There was movement in Merritt's kitchen, female voices chattering excitedly. He couldn't hear what they were saying.

For once in his life, he didn't know what cards to play. Couldn't see an obvious next move.

There's always tomorrow. And the day after . . .

Merritt's anticipation for the wedding tomorrow had been bright enough to light up the night, but all he felt standing beside her was coldness. And fear.

He ran a shaking hand down his face. Remembered that the town marshal was inside. She'd keep Merritt from harm, at least for a while.

Jack snuck back the way he'd come, then down the street that would take him back along the boardwalk.

He had a terrible urge to return to the work site. What if Morris had undone all the clearing Jack had done today?

He'd told himself he could make this work. He could give up his nomadic ways, could try and be a good husband to her, make a life here.

Who was he kidding?

He hadn't even been able to get the words out.

I'm not your John.

He was a no-good coward. One who'd brought trouble to her door.

He was walking in front of the dance hall when two man-sized shadows separated from the building, jumping toward him.

Jack's stomach plunged as he recognized Morris's hat, though he couldn't make out the man's face in the darkness.

Jack reached for his gun, his anger at what had happened to Merritt spurring him on—

But Morris didn't wait. He slugged Jack in the stomach. Pain splintered through his insides and he doubled over.

Morris wasn't done yet. He followed with a fist to Jack's right cheek, making him see stars.

The memory of Merritt thrown to the ground, her tiny gasp of pain, shivered through Jack's mind.

He roared, throwing himself at Morris. He landed a punch to the man's face, heard a satisfying crunch.

But he hadn't counted on being outnumbered and took an elbow to the mouth from somewhere beside him.

Jack tasted the coppery tang of blood, felt warmth slide down his chin. His arm was wrenched behind him and then trapped there as Morris leaned into Jack's shoulders and pinned him against the door. He had a good thirty pounds on Jack, and suddenly, Jack couldn't breathe.

The second man hovered behind Morris, his eyes narrowed. It was Burns. Jack's worlds collided as the man smirked a twisted smile.

"Henshaw wants his five hundred bucks back, you cheater." Morris breathed the words into Jack's face, his breath foul with stale cigar smoke. He reeked of whiskey.

"It was two hundred," Jack gasped with what little air he had left. "And it's gone."

He tried to get in a punch at Morris's midsection, but the other man was too close, and Jack had no leverage.

Jack's hand slipped toward the revolver in his belt.

"Watch him," Burns growled.

Morris knocked Jack's hand away.

"I don't know what kind of game you're playing with the little schoolmarm," Morris said, "but I want the money."

Jack struggled harder, even as his breath locked in his chest made dark spots dance at the edges of his vision. "It's gone," he repeated.

"You got twenty-four hours to get it back," Morris said.

He shoved against Jack's windpipe and then released him slightly. "Otherwise, your pretty schoolmarm is the one who gets roughed up."

He shoved Jack, knocking him into the doorknob. The door gave way—maybe it had already been open—and Jack couldn't gain his balance, as lightheaded as he was. He fell, knocking his hip, and a sharp pain shot through his elbow as he hit the ground. His hat flew off, landing somewhere in the darkness.

He struggled for breath as the two sets of footsteps faded away. Every inhale burned.

What was he going to do? They'd threatened Merritt, and Jack couldn't get that money back.

He'd won it fair and square. No cheating involved.

But a hired gun like Morris wouldn't care about that. He'd take out the declared debt in flesh.

And Jack couldn't let that happen.

He pushed up to his knees, his entire side aching. He wrapped one arm around it, was close enough to one of the tables to drag himself to his feet with the other.

The clouds must've parted. Moonlight streamed in the open doorway, and Jack glimpsed the jagged tears through the three backdrops he and the children had so painstakingly painted.

They were shredded, as if they'd been slashed with a knife.

There would be no repairing them. No replacing them, not with the pageant on Monday.

Morris had threatened to hurt Merritt physically, but this was enough to ruin the pageant—and her career.

Jack felt sick. Coldness seeped through his skin, but inside he felt like he was burning up.

He'd done this. Not directly, but Merritt would suffer because of him.

He collected his hat and fled the room, pulling the door closed behind him—little good that it would do. Was the town really so secure that no one thought to lock this door?

Jack felt the cold wind cut through him and realized his coat was open. Numbness stole over him, and it wasn't until he heard the distant train whistle that he realized what he needed to do.

He found himself on the platform minutes later. Another whistle, this one closer.

He hadn't checked the train schedule in days, but if memory served, there was a quick late-night stop. He had fifty cents in his pocket. Enough for a ticket. Didn't matter the destination.

The platform was deserted, the cold wind buffeting him.

He mashed his hat further down on his head. Touching the brim reminded him of Merritt, of those moments when she'd given him the hat. The way she'd looked at him.

Like he mattered, her eyes shining like he was some prince.

If he left, surely Morris would follow him.

Unless . . . would Jack's leaving make Merritt more of a target?

The thought of putting her in deeper danger tore him apart from the inside out. The wound on his face pulsed with pain, but it was nothing compared to the thought of that thug getting his hands on her.

She had Danna to protect her. They were close friends.

I can help you. The marshal's words rang through his head. But Danna had an entire town to protect.

I'm coming to know you. Merritt's words from yesterday ripped through him, and he leaned against the side of the station for support as the train chugged into place with a last squeal of brakes and a hiss of steam.

She didn't know him. Not really. He'd kept his true self from her. She didn't even know his name.

She might think she cared about him, but it was only an illusion. It wasn't real.

Leaving was for the best. It was the only thing he could do to try and keep her safe.

Wasn't it?

Eleven

ERRITT STOOD IN THE PREACHER'S
parlor, wearing her new dress.

In the silence, all she could hear was her own breath and the ticking of a clock on the mantel.

Her eyes flicked to the clock once more, and she forced them away, but not before she saw the time had ticked another minute from the day.

"I'm sure your young man will be along shortly," Mrs. Carson said. She stood up from the settee where she'd perched moments ago. "Would you like a cup of coffee?"

"No, thank you."

Mrs. Carson bustled into the kitchen, leaving Merritt alone in the parlor.

Jack was late.

Merritt's stomach twisted and she pressed her palm there to try and steady herself.

He wasn't *that* late. Only a few minutes.

The preacher himself had waited with her and Mrs. Carson in the parlor until five after and then excused himself to his office. Merritt could hear him muttering to himself and the sound of pages turning. Service would be starting soon, the church building a half block away.

Where was Jack?

She remembered the way Jack had looked at her when he'd seen her in this dress. Like it was Christmas morning and he'd just received everything he wanted.

Like she was beautiful.

But where was he?

Another memory surfaced, this one of his stillness last night when she'd moved to kiss him goodbye in the darkness outside his house. They'd only had a scarce few moments together after she'd been knocked off the boardwalk, and she'd been shaken and a little discombobulated, reassured by his arm around her shoulders and his strength at her side.

Had he been shaken too?

I need to tell you—

He'd been trying to tell her something, while she'd been excitedly prattling on about the auction and donations. And then her friends had been waiting for her.

Perhaps she should've invited him inside.

Nerves slithered through her stomach like a knot of snakes. What had Jack wanted to tell her?

Where was he?

A shadow passed by the sunshine-filled window and her heart leaped.

A knock sounded at the door, and she worked to steady her breathing. That was Jack. He was late, but he was here.

The preacher's wife came in from the kitchen and shot a harried smile at Merritt, then opened the door to reveal the person on the other side.

Danna.

Merritt felt a rush of trepidation as her heart pounded. Danna would only have come if something was wrong.

"Where's Jack? What's happened?" Merritt hated the way her voice wavered.

Danna scanned the room the way Merritt had seen her do before, as if she were on the lookout for danger. "He's not here?"

Merritt shook her head.

Danna nodded to Mrs. Carson. "Would you give us a minute?"

The older woman sent a sympathetic glance to Merritt. "Of course." The woman joined her husband in his office.

Danna strode into the room and motioned to the settee where the preacher's wife had previously sat. "Why don't you sit down."

"I don't want to." But that quaver remained in her voice, and Merritt took the two steps that put her in front of the settee and sat down on it.

Danna took the chair across. She looked grim.

"Just tell me. Is Jack all right? Is he injured?"

"How much do you know about Jack?" Danna asked.

What did that have to do with Jack's whereabouts? Her hands fluttered in her lap. "What he wrote me in his letters." She had a flash of Jack's expression as a reflection in the kitchen window when he'd told her about losing his brother. "And he's told me a little more."

"You heard the name Jack Easton?"

Jack.

But she didn't know the surname Easton.

Merritt shook her head stiffly. "Who-who is that?"

If anything, the grim frown on Danna's face intensified. "Jack Easton is a gambler. He's somewhat famous in these parts."

From the way Danna glanced to the side, Merritt knew there was more she wasn't saying.

"Tell me."

"There's been a man asking for Jack Easton around town. Rumor is, he's a hired gun. Is it possible he's looking for your Jack?"

Cold seeped along the edges of Merritt's extremities, shivered down her spine. She wiped her cheek, surprised to find a stray tear there. She wasn't crying, was she?

"No—no. Jack is a *businessman*."

There was movement from the other room, and Danna sat back in her chair when the preacher walked into the parlor, followed by his wife.

"Miss Harding, I'm sorry but I have to go now. If your young man arrives, you can wait here. There'll be time for the ceremony after service." Mr. and Mrs. Carson slipped out the door, looking uncomfortable.

Merritt took a shaky breath. She felt battered from all sides. Jack was supposed to be here. Why hadn't he come? And she couldn't make sense of what Danna was saying.

And now the time for her wedding to Jack had come and gone.

She wasn't getting married this morning.

The reality blasted into her like a burst from the fire she'd helped fight days ago.

Jack wasn't coming.

There'd be no ceremony, no sacred moments standing face-to-face with Jack while they recited their vows.

No quiet nights spent in conversation over the supper table.

No future children.

Her dreams were crumbling around her.

And Jack hadn't said a word.

Or had he?

Was this what he'd been trying to tell her last night, in the rush of activity? That he couldn't marry her?

She blinked Danna into focus when her friend leaned forward in the chair with her elbows on her knees. "Is there any chance that your Jack, your John, is the same man as Jack Easton?"

More tears seeped down Merritt's face, and she reached into her pocket for a handkerchief—but then remembered she hadn't brought one. She'd thought this morning would be a time of joy.

Danna looked slightly panicked in the face of Merritt's tears and scrambled in her own pockets until she found a handkerchief. She pushed it into Merritt's hands.

Merritt wiped her face, tried to focus on Danna's question, though she felt unsettled from her head to her toes.

"How could John be Jack? Are you saying that this gambler wrote me letters, posing as a businessman? Why?"

Danna's expression was as puzzled as Merritt felt. "I was hoping he'd be here, that he could answer those questions for me." Then her expression darkened. "There's more." She sighed. "There's no easy way to tell you this, but there appears to have been a break-in at the dance hall last night."

The dance hall? No.

Danna continued, though Merritt was shaking her head. "The tables and chairs weren't touched, but someone took a knife to your backdrops."

The pageant backdrops. "H-how bad? Maybe we can repair them—"

Now Danna was the one shaking her head. "It's bad. Beyond repair. As if someone was . . . taking revenge."

Merritt thought of what Jack had said about Mr. Polk working with Billy Burns. Surely Mr. Polk wouldn't have done something like this. But who—

She buried her face in her hands. None of it made sense, and she felt raw all over, like she'd been scrubbed with harsh lye soap over every inch of her body.

There was a knock on the door, and it opened before either she or Danna could move.

Her heart leaped as she registered Jack standing there. He'd come!

But her eyes took in all the details. He had a bruise on one cheek, and there was a rip in his shirt beneath his coat.

It was his expression that arrested her, had her sticking to her seat when her heart told her to go to him.

He looked beaten. Resigned, somehow.

This wasn't a groom anticipating his wedding ceremony.

His gaze skittered away from Merritt, as if it was easier to look at Danna. "I don't know how much you've figured out, but I'm not John Crosby."

Jack couldn't bear to look at Merritt. She was wearing *that* dress, but her face was tearstained, her eyes wide with hurt.

He could barely hold the marshal's gaze. It'd felt almost impossible for him to make his feet carry him here this morning.

There was a part of him that had hoped he'd find Merritt already gone. Given up on him.

But lady luck wasn't in his corner on this one.

He edged into the room, holding his hat at his side. Closed the door, though he wanted to run out of it.

"I am Jack Easton," he said. "Not John Crosby."

He'd said the same to two members of the school board just this morning after he'd convinced them to meet with him. He'd spent over an hour with them, explaining what he'd heard and how Merritt's job had been threatened. What part he'd played and why.

The preacher had spent all week trying to convince Jack that there was a God up there listening. Jack still didn't know whether he believed it, but he'd sent up a prayer, such as it was, that what he'd said would make a difference. For her.

Merritt loved those kids. Loved her job. He couldn't be a part of taking that away from her.

Danna stood from her chair, stuffing her hands in her pockets. "I'll go—"

"You should stay," he interrupted. "Part of what I've got to say involves the marshal's office." And he knew she and Merritt were close. Merritt would want a friend, surely.

"Did you—did you write me those letters, pretending to be John?" Merritt stood up too, and he saw the tremble in her hands before she clenched them at her sides.

"No." He was ashamed to admit what he'd done, now that he knew her, knew what she'd think about his omissions. "When I got off the train, I was—someone was following me. You assumed I was John, and I thought I could pretend for a couple of hours and leave town."

His gaze had been drawn to her, and he saw the realization dawning in her eyes. She hadn't wanted to believe he wasn't John, and it was hitting her hard.

She sat back down, turning her face to look at the wall.

He felt like he'd been slugged by Morris all over again.

"What happened to the real John?" Danna demanded. There was the marshal in her voice, wondering if Jack had caused trouble. An echo of Mrs. Farr's voice played in his mind. *What'd you do now?* But he shoved down the roiling in his stomach to answer.

"I was riding in the same train car with him. Overheard him conversing with another passenger. He had cold feet." There was no easy way to say it, but he saw Merritt flinch, even though her face was turned.

"You could probably send a wire," he told Danna. "Verify that he's alive and well."

Surreptitiously, Merritt dabbed her face with a handkerchief.

"I'm sorry," he said. The words felt empty. Not enough. "Deceiving you was wrong, and—I have no excuse."

None except that he'd fallen for her. That painful realization was what had propelled him off the train platform last night, sent him to see the school board members this morning to try and right things for her.

She mattered in a way nothing had for a long time.

He turned the hat in his hands and shifted his feet. He'd come clean, finally. Told her the truth about who he really was.

But he didn't feel any relief.

So maybe it was time to go.

She twisted on the settee until she was facing him, and now her eyes were blazing. "Why'd you stay?" she demanded, her voice like ice. "You'd planned to leave that first night. Why didn't you?"

He felt the same visceral tug in his gut that he had that night when she'd flung herself into his arms and he'd held her.

It was a pull to *her*. To the one woman he'd let get close, who had kept him in Calvin.

But looking at her tear-matted lashes and the streaks of red in her cheeks, the fist around her handkerchief and the clear anger shining in her eyes, he couldn't say that.

"I thought I could help," he said instead. "I didn't want you to lose your school, your job. I wanted—" He shrugged helplessly. He didn't know what he'd wanted.

Not to hurt her.

If there was any way to take away the hurt he knew he'd caused, he would take it. "Every moment spent with you is one I'll treasure."

She turned her face at his words, as if she couldn't bear to look at him.

He felt the pulse of pain, more than that blow of Morris's to his liver. This was it.

"Where'd you get that bruise?" Danna asked.

His gaze flicked to her. He'd almost forgotten she was present.

"A hired gun by the name of Morris." It was easier to focus on the marshal than Merritt when he felt like he was burning up inside. "He's been looking for me. Claims I cheated at cards."

"Did you?"

He didn't blink. "I don't cheat. Don't have to." He went on. "Morris demanded a sum of money that I won in a card game. I don't have it anymore." He tipped his head toward Merritt. "He'd seen us together and made some threats. He's the one who slashed the backdrops."

Merritt flinched but didn't seem surprised. So, she knew.

That was enough, wasn't it? He'd told Merritt the truth. Warned Danna of the threats.

"I'm leaving on the next train."

There was an awkward pause. He didn't know what he'd hoped she would say. Something. Anything.

But she kept her face turned away, and she didn't owe him one red cent.

He took a few steps forward, a prickling awareness of the marshal watching his every move slithering up the back of his neck. Did she see the slight limp from where Burns had landed that lucky punch? Every muscle felt tight and sore.

Jack placed the hat on the settee within arm's reach of Merritt. "I can't keep this. It wouldn't be right. I'm—I'm sorry for everything."

He would never forget those moments of breathless wonder when she'd given him the gift—but it had never been meant for him. Not Jack. She'd wanted John this entire time.

He strode out of the parlor and closed the door behind him.

He'd hesitated for a moment too long, because he heard the sound of her muffled sob from inside.

He'd made Merritt cry.

He rested one hand against the doorframe, leaning his face into his bent arm. The movement made every sore muscle in his abdomen pull.

There was a part of him grateful for the pain. He deserved it, didn't he? For years, he'd prided himself on fixing problems. Saving the miners' widows from having their homes foreclosed on. Providing funds for an orphanage.

Jack had believed that righting wrongs would fix what was wrong with him.

But this time, his motives hadn't been pure.

He'd let his heart get involved. It'd only taken one conversation over supper that first night for him to see how special Merritt was.

He'd let himself believe there was a chance for him to be with Merritt.

He knew better.

The odds of one ace being drawn after another were longer than a Texas prairie.

Jack's chances of someone like Merritt falling in love with him were even longer than that.

He'd acted liked one of the saps who shouldn't play cards, hoping for the one-in-a-million chance to win.

Jack forced himself to move away from the door, from the sound of her quiet crying. He was getting on that train. He'd told the school board members he was leaving town. Stopped in at the mercantile and the grocer and spread the word there. Tried to ignore the shock and whispers he'd left behind him.

He couldn't let himself care. The important thing was ensuring Merritt's safety. If Morris came looking for Jack, surely someone would tell the hired gun that Jack was gone.

Jack looked over his shoulder at the preacher's tidy home. For a moment, he wished things had been different. That he'd walked into town and met Merritt under different circumstances.

But the part of him that couldn't lie to himself knew it wouldn't have made any difference.

She never would've chosen him. Jack Easton. Gambler. Loner. Orphan.

She deserved someone better.

And he wasn't it.

Twelve

DAYS AGO, THE TRAIN COMPARTMENT
had been nearly empty. This afternoon's journey was
the opposite: the car had only a handful of empty seats.
Jack found himself in an aisle seat, next to a portly woman
who was balancing three brown-wrapped packages in her
lap and had a carpetbag between her feet.

Across the aisle, a man who must have been around Jack's
age held a young boy in his lap while a girl of six sat next
to him at the window, swinging her feet.

Jack held a newspaper, folded into quarters. He forced
his eyes to scan the tiny type, though the ache in his head
made it difficult to concentrate.

He'd been hoping for an answer in the paper's pages.
Where was he supposed to end up next?

He needed the focus of a job. A new mission. Something
to distract him.

Across the aisle, the little girl was whispering urgently to her father, who looked harried but then sighed. He stood up, juggling the boy in his arms.

"I don't gotta use the water closet!" shouted the young boy.

One or two heads turned at the commotion, but mostly folks were absorbed in their own conversations or didn't seem to care.

The father put the boy in the seat where he had been sitting. The little girl had moved out into the aisle and was dancing in place.

"Stay in this seat," the man said sternly. "You understand?"

The boy nodded, eyes wide with sincerity.

Jack snapped his paper, blinking his eyes into focus.

He didn't care about a little family traveling on the train. Why should he?

The ache from the bruise in his side seemed to pulse.

It was far too easy to imagine Merritt holding a toddler on her hip or comforting a child with a skinned knee.

She'd be such a good mother.

His head ached when he pictured another man in that scene with Merritt. Imagined her looking at someone else the way she'd looked at him, like he was some kind of hero. Like he'd hung the moon. Bitterness coated his tongue.

The little boy across the aisle hadn't sat still after all. He was standing on the seat his father had left him in, facing backward. He seemed to be looking for his father, and Jack found himself craning his neck to try to see the man too.

There were several people crowded at the end of the car. None of them was the boy's father.

The rack above the family's row of seats was stuffed with passengers' bags and parcels. Some soul had left their bag with a long leather strap hanging down. It swung slightly with the sway of the train's movement and seemed to tempt the boy, even though it was at least a foot out of his reach overhead.

Jack could see that the bag was wedged behind another, larger suitcase.

The boy stuck his tongue out of the corner of his mouth in concentration and scrambled to climb on the back of the seat, craning his head to keep the strap in view.

Jack sent another glance over his shoulder. No father in sight. None of the other passengers seated around them seemed to notice or care that the boy might fall from his precarious position or that if he did tug on that leather strap, something from the overstuffed rack might fall on top of him.

Jack sighed.

It wasn't his business.

But—

"Kid, your pa told you to sit down."

The child pretended not to hear him, still completely focused on the strap. He couldn't reach it. There were still several inches of empty air above his hand.

But then he pushed off the seat back and flung himself into the air.

Jack reacted without thinking, standing to brace one hand on the luggage overhead while his other arm came around the boy, who'd managed to pull on the strap but had lost his grip and was tumbling toward the aisle.

"Hey!"

Jack quickly set the boy on his feet in the seat, aware of the father's presence behind him. He stepped back into the crowded space in front of his own seat, bracing for angry words or a physical confrontation.

But the man nudged his daughter into her seat and slumped into his own, putting the boy on the ground between his knees.

"I told you to sit still," the father told his son and then nodded toward Jack. "Thank you for catching him. He might've been crushed if he'd knocked all that luggage down."

Jack nodded.

"You got kids of your own?"

The image of Merritt holding a baby of her own jumped into Jack's mind. He shook his head.

"No? I thought I recognized that long face. I've seen it in the mirror enough lately. You missin' your family?"

Jack's chest squeezed tighter. "I don't have any family."

He lifted his newspaper, hoping to end the conversation.

The little boy squirmed, trying to nudge past his father and into the aisle. The father, more patient than Jack, diverted his son's attention to something passing outside the window, and the boy went to stand in the space next to his sister's feet, peering out the wavy glass.

"My wife's been with her sister for a coupla weeks," the man said. "Cecil Treadway," he introduced himself, and Jack did the same.

"Her sister was in the family way but lost the baby, and my Jeannie went to be with her. She doesn't know we're coming." Cecil sounded proud of that. "Her last letter said how much she missed the kids. And we all miss her too. So we're gonna surprise her for Christmas, stay a day or two to pick up her spirits."

Jack nodded along, but his eyes had dropped. Cecil was obviously a family man through and through. He cared about his wife, about his kids. He hadn't gotten angry when his boy had done something naughty.

What was wrong with Jack that he'd never had a family to love him? He was envious of a little kid—a stranger on a train.

"You look like I did before I got my life straightened out and convinced Jeannie to marry me."

Jack didn't know what he'd done to invite Cecil into this personal conversation, but found himself frowning. "I don't have a woman. I don't have anyone."

"Hmm."

Jack suddenly realized, after years of gambling, that he'd clenched his fist on his knee—a tell.

"It would never work between us." He practically growled the words to this stranger. "Our lives are too different."

"So change."

Cecil said the words in a matter-of-fact way, as if doing so was as easy as a snap of Jack's fingers. How was he to make a living if he didn't visit a poker table?

Jack didn't know whether he could be content living in one place. He thought of the way all of Merritt's friends, her community, had pitched in to help when she'd needed it.

Thought of the lonely nights he'd spent lying in bed in a different hotel than the night before.

He'd told himself it was what he wanted, being anchorless. Having nothing to tie him down.

But now he saw the emptiness of the life he'd been living.

Merritt had seen an empty future stretching before her, and she'd taken action. Not run away from it.

"What if I'm not worthy of her?" His voice sounded rough, and he saw a flash of surprise in Cecil's eyes.

"You ever heard of the Good Book?"

He'd sat through several hours of Mr. Carson reading him stories, explaining what they meant. The prodigal son, with his father waiting for the lost son to return. The road to Jericho. Jesus.

They weren't the stories Mrs. Farr had told Jack when she'd raised the belt to punish him.

Jack had promised himself he'd let Carson's stories filter over him like water over a stone in a creek.

But Cecil's question brought everything he'd heard this week into sharp relief.

"None of us are worthy," Cecil said. "Not without the sacrifice Jesus made for us."

Jack felt the truth of it settle in his bones. Mrs. Farr had been wrong. God wasn't a cruel taskmaster or waiting for Jack to make a mistake.

He'd sent His Son to earth to make it possible for Jack to be worthy.

He sat with the realization, with the tears that smarted his eyes, for long moments while the noise of the train car faded into the background.

When he looked back to Cecil, the other man was smiling patiently.

"Thank you," Jack said. "I needed to hear that."

"Ain't it funny how God's Providence put us on this train together?"

It was something, all right.

"I got one more question for you."

Jack nodded for him to continue.

"Did you tell her you loved her? Your girl?"

No. He'd been too much of a coward to show his feelings when he'd seen the hurt he'd caused.

"Maybe you should."

Merritt heard a shuffle of feet as she tugged another hardback chair into perfect alignment with its neighbor.

She glanced up to see Corrine and Danna walk into the dance hall.

The compassion on her friends' expressions was too much to bear, and she gave an impatient sniff as she moved a step forward and rearranged another chair.

Merritt had counted earlier, but she turned to the front of the room and began to count the chairs all over again. It gave her an excuse not to face her friends directly. The signs of her tears from earlier had faded. No more splotchy cheeks or red tip of her nose.

She was fine.

"Have you eaten lunch?" Corrine asked.

" . . . forty-five, forty-six—just a moment," she called to her friend. More counting, the rhythm a constant in her head. Sixty chairs.

It was more space than she'd had last year in the classroom, when families had squished together, most standing, to see their children perform.

She glanced regretfully at the plain blue backdrop, hastily assembled and painted after she'd left the preacher's home this morning. The room still smelled of paint, and they wouldn't have the scene for the manger, but it would have to do.

Thinking of the destruction of the beautiful artwork that had been made by her students and Jack made her angry.

She moved through the rows of perfectly straight chairs to the tables she'd dragged to one side of the room.

Danna's and Corrine's footsteps rang out as they trailed her across the room.

"How can we help?" Corrine asked carefully.

"I think everything is in order," Merritt said with a falsely cheerful note to her voice. She wished they would just go away.

She caught sight of the haphazard way the auction pieces were displayed. That simply wouldn't do.

She began to straighten them, wrinkling her nose as she tried to decide whether to sit up or lay down the porcelain doll donated by the mercantile.

"Merritt." She'd heard a gentle tone in Danna's usually strident voice only once before—when the marshal had been attempting to comfort a young child who had witnessed a tragedy.

Merritt found it easier to focus on the small changes to the auction items than face her friends. She was fine, after all.

"Stop," Corrine commanded, and now there was an impatient snap to her voice.

When Merritt reached for the next piece, a black hat that reminded her of Jack with a piercing intensity, Corrine stepped forward and gripped her forearm. "Merritt!"

Merritt felt a little breathless when she faced her friends, her eyes instantly smarting. She didn't want to cry anymore.

"We want to talk to you about Jack," Danna said gently.

Merritt pressed her lips together to keep them from shaking. "There's nothing to talk about. He lied to me. He wasn't my groom after all."

There was no husband for her. No future children. Only a classroom and work, work, work . . .

Corrine squeezed her arm. "When my first husband died, I felt . . . well, I felt a lot of things. Relief. Guilt. I started to sink into loneliness, but it was you who reminded me that God is always with me—husband or no husband."

Had it been almost two years ago? Merritt remembered evenings spent with Corrine when Corrine had been a widow with a newborn and toddler. She couldn't tell the other woman what she'd said back then. *God is always with me.* She might've said that.

But right now the words felt like a scrape against raw skin.

She caught sight of the children's costumes, lying neatly over the back row of chairs, waiting for her students to arrive. One white angel's robe had slipped and pooled in the seat of the chair. She slipped past her friends, ignoring the look they exchanged, and went to straighten it.

She'd been a fool to think she needed more than this.

What was so wrong with getting a little lost in her work? She was needed here. A teacher was always needed.

Danna sidled up next to her, reaching out to touch one of the angel wings. "There were times in my marriage to Fred that I felt lonely. A husband isn't a guarantee that you'll never feel that way. It wasn't until I realized I had to find my contentment in God that I truly found peace."

A shudder passed through Merritt as realization washed over her. She'd kept her plans to marry John Crosby from her family and friends because she hadn't wanted to admit how lonely she'd become. She'd allowed herself to become lost in her job and then in the idea of having a husband of her own.

She should've been looking for peace from her Heavenly Father. And it wasn't too late to start searching, was it?

Danna cleared her throat, then changed the subject. "I got hold of some interesting information when I wired the marshal back in Nevada."

Merritt shook her head. She didn't know whether she could hear any news about Jack, and that must be what Danna was talking about.

"Rumor is Jack won a large sum at the poker tables. Nearly bankrupted a grocer who was charging higher prices to some of the folks in town—folks who mostly seemed to be immigrants, if you catch my meaning."

Merritt's heart squeezed. *I was trying to protect you.* He'd said the words to her, and she would never be able to forget the man who'd once been a boy, who'd tried and failed to save his best friend and adopted brother. Of course Jack would've tried to right the wrong.

"The marshal said those same folks came into some money. Seven families in all. None of them would say where they'd gotten the cash."

A tear slipped down Merritt's cheek.

"Also heard from the sheriff over in Colorado, where this Morris fellow is from. He's a hired gun mostly working with a silver miner there. Big operation, bad working conditions. Several men died in a cave-in. And their widows mysteriously came into some money after Jack left town there. After he won a big pot in a hand of five card draw."

Merritt swiped at the tears on her cheeks. Her hollow stomach rumbled. She'd skipped lunch. Maybe she should go home and find something to eat.

"He sounds like the hero from the play you wrote when we were children. The one based off that Robin Hood book," Corrine murmured. "As I recall, you made me the Little John character."

If Jack had done those things, it did sound like someone stealing from the rich to serve the poor. Jack wasn't a fictional character. But that didn't mean he wasn't heroic.

Could one be heroic and be a liar at the same time?

Her emotions were muddled. Her thoughts, too. Jack had cleared away most of the rubble so the school building could be rebuilt. He'd hauled auction donations to her house.

Then we gotta talk.

I need to tell you—

Had Jack tried to tell her the truth? There'd been times she'd sensed something building up between them, on the cusp of being shared.

If she blinked, she'd see the stricken expression when she'd given him the hat box.

I've never been given a Christmas gift before . . .

Corrine came close and put her arm around Merritt's shoulders. Only last night, they'd giggled together as they'd whispered what next Christmas might be like with Merritt as a married woman.

"I let myself get lost in him," Merritt whispered. "I should've known—how could I not have noticed that he wasn't John?"

He'd told her from the beginning. *Call me Jack.*

She felt so foolish.

"You fell in love with him," Danna said softly.

Merritt shook her head, but she couldn't deny it out loud. She had. She'd fallen for Jack. The man with the pirate's smile. The man who'd once been a boy who had desperately wanted a family and found hardship instead.

She blinked against more tears that threatened to fall. There'd been too many realizations in too short a time. She needed space to think. Time. And she didn't have that, not with the pageant and auction looming close.

She smiled a trembling smile at her friends. "I have to finish getting things ready."

Danna's eyes showed the compassion she felt.

Corrine squeezed Merritt's hand. "We'll help."

Merritt didn't know what God had in store for her. But she had friends beside her who hadn't let her forget that God truly loved her.

Thirteen

I T WAS FINISHED.

Merritt leaned her hip against the auction table with the last of the sold items atop it.

Mr. Castlerock and his bank manager, Mr. Silverton, stood at the back of the dance hall, collecting money from those who had won the bid for each item. In a few moments, they would take the cash down to the bank for safekeeping.

Over the past few minutes, as the auction had wrapped up, Merritt's students had trailed to the back of the room, and now they were slipping on their costumes so the pageant could begin.

The auction, and Castlerock's matching donation, had raised enough money for the lumber and nails and roofing material to rebuild the school.

The limited funds wouldn't provide desks or materials for the students to study, but Merritt trusted God to provide those things when the time was right. She'd come to a tentative sort of peace last night, after reading Scripture and praying for God to fill the empty hole in her heart.

But watching the auction items sell, knowing that Jack had been the one to help procure them, brought back every ounce of yearning.

With a pang from her broken heart, she pushed the thoughts of Jack from her mind. Now wasn't the time.

Mr. Castlerock called out the final total, and there was a cheer from the students, followed by roaring applause from their parents.

Daniel hurried over to where Merritt stood, followed by his father in a fine suit.

"Three cheers for our intrepid schoolteacher," Daniel's father called out with his hand at his mouth to amplify the words.

Heat blasted into her cheeks as cheers rang out among children and parents, even some of the grandparents and townsfolk who'd attended. Feet stomped the floor.

She caught Mr. Castlerock's eye and he nodded to her. She waved. He and Mr. Silverton left with the money safe and sound, and she was left to soak up the raucous cheers.

She quieted the crowd, urging the students to finish their preparations for the pageant, and moved to the front of the room they'd designated as a stage, thoughts noodling at the back of her mind all the while.

She loved moments like these—being a teacher when the children were excited to learn and work together.

But the longing that had prompted her to send an answer

to that mail-order bride ad remained. She wanted a family. Children of her own. A husband who loved her.

She wanted Jack.

Right now, she would have to lean on God's promises of comfort, promises that He would never forsake her. In time, God might change her heart.

As some of the children slipped down the aisle between. the seats and stepped up onto the raised platform that was their makeshift stage, she couldn't stop the thoughts from slipping into her heart and taking hold.

She missed Jack.

Maybe he wasn't John, and maybe he'd never meant to come here at all, or to stay, but something had happened when he'd stepped off that train.

After tonight, her obligations to the children would be over for a week. There would be no school over Christmas, to allow the children to be with their families.

Was there a way Merritt could track down Jack? Find him? Talk to him?

She forced the intruding thoughts away, tried to focus. The children had worked hard memorizing lines, and she found herself mouthing the words along with them.

Until the back doors to the dance hall slammed open.

Heads turned as a hulking man in a black slicker entered.

Harriet stood in the center of the stage and faltered her line, trailing off with wide eyes.

"Where's Jack Easton?" the stranger bellowed.

Quiet murmurs broke out in the crowd, and one man, sitting on the aisle, stood up to block his progress.

"There are children—"

Morris—because this had to be the man Jack had told Merritt and Danna about—slugged him so hard in the stomach that he collapsed to the ground. Terror streaked through Merritt. A woman screamed.

"Run," she whispered to the nearest child, gripping Clarissa's shoulder briefly. "Upstairs, quick."

She shuffled to the front of the platform, nudging and pushing each child, snapping them out of their terror so that they ran or crawled off the stage and scampered to the stairwell, half hidden on the rear wall.

It was only a modicum of safety. Upstairs was a small loft.

Morris's eyes flashed and trained on her.

Someone shouted, "Get the marshal!" from the back of the room.

Morris didn't even look at them, only flipped both sides of his coat open to reveal a pair of bone-handled revolvers strapped to his waist. A clear threat.

"Nobody leaves."

He stopped in front of her. Standing at the front corner of the stage, she was a half foot taller than him, but she was caught in his stare like a mouse trapped by the hypnotizing gaze of a cobra.

"Where's Jack?" he demanded.

"Gone." And she was glad of it.

She'd noticed the way Jack had walked out of the Carsons' home earlier, favoring his left side. And that bruise on his cheek . . .

She hated the man in front of her for hurting Jack.

"Then I guess you're my collateral. You're coming with me—"

There was movement somewhere in the crowd—she caught it from her peripheral vision. Morris's head turned even as he reached for his gun with his right hand.

"Leave the lady alone. It's me you want."

Merritt gasped softly as Jack sauntered down the stairs she'd just sent her students up. He was still hatless, his shirt collar wrinkled. Smirking. An arrogant tilt to his head that she'd never seen before. This was the gambler Danna had described to Merritt.

Morris rattled off a curse word, making her jump. For a few seconds, she'd been focused on Jack, soaking up the sight of him, but her pounding heart and shaking limbs hadn't let her forget the danger lurking only feet away.

Jack's eyes flicked to somewhere in the front row of seats as his boots hit the floor. Morris took two steps toward him.

"Why don't we play a game?" Jack asked. His voice was completely calm and unruffled. Merritt realized he held a deck of cards, casually passing them between his hands with a sound like a shuffle.

Jack kept moving, slower now, toward Morris.

"I'll cut the deck once. Then you cut it."

It was only because she couldn't tear her eyes away that she saw the minute nod. Who was Jack nodding to?

"Whoever draws the higher card wins. I win, and you leave and never come back."

Morris shook his head. "I don't gamble—"

But Jack twisted his hand, and every card in the deck flew toward Morris's face.

The split second of distraction, when the bigger man

batted at the flying cards, was enough for Jack to lunge at him. A man came off the front row of chairs, tackling Morris's booted feet.

Morris was thrown off-balance, and when Jack pummeled him, he was knocked to the floor.

But he roared, and Merritt knew he wasn't done fighting yet. She was terrified he'd reach for one of his guns.

"Merritt, get outta here!" Jack grunted.

Someone pulled her off the stage, and she lost sight of the tussle.

"That's enough!" Danna's strong voice rang out, and she strode through the doors, flanked by two deputies with their guns drawn. They ran to the front, training their guns on Morris.

Danna tapped Jack's shoulder, and he sat back on his haunches as Morris put his hands over his head.

Merritt stood on trembling legs and saw the trickle of blood below Jack's nose before he wiped it away. Jack's eyes searched the crowd and settled when they caught hers.

And then one of Danna's deputies stepped between them, reaching down to disarm Morris.

Morris was shouting and swearing, and Merritt glanced at the stairs to see little feet and the hems of costumes on the top few steps. The children must be terrified.

"I'll get them," the nearest mother murmured, heading that way.

"We're gonna take this outside, you hear?" Danna said to Morris, who stood between the two deputies, expression belligerent.

Danna looked around the room and waved for Merritt to accompany them.

She trailed the three lawmen and Jack, who walked slightly in front of her with an air of tension.

He'd come back. But why?

On the boardwalk, darkness encompassed them. She shivered in the cold, having left her cape inside, but sidled next to Jack anyway.

The two deputies kept Morris between them. Danna faced him directly. "We can do this here and now, or we can do this over at the jail, with you in a cell. You threatened a young woman and caused a public disturbance."

"Ain't no need for that," Morris growled, "s'long as Jack gives me the money he owes my boss." His evil gaze flicked to Jack, and he spat in his direction. "You cheated him out of it."

Jack didn't react outwardly. "I never cheat. There were three other men at the table with us. Witnesses that I obtained my winnings fairly."

"You got a name for those men?" Danna asked.

Jack rattled off three names unfamiliar to Merritt.

"What'd you do with the money?" Danna asked.

Now there was a hesitation from Jack. "I gave it away," he finally said.

"Liar!"

One of the deputies put his hand on Morris when the man would've lunged for Jack.

"I can verify Mr. Easton's story," Danna said. "With witnesses, your boss would've known his accusation of cheating wouldn't hold water with a judge."

So he'd sent this hired muscle.

Merritt shivered again, and Jack's eyes skittered to her and then away. He shrugged out of his coat and held it out in front of him as if he needed her permission to give it to her.

As if they were strangers.

She looked at him, emotion overflowing in her eyes, and then turned to offer him her back.

There was only a beat of hesitation before he put it over her shoulders.

His familiar warmth and scent enveloped her, and she sent a prayer winging heavenward. *Please let Jack have come back to stay.*

Danna continued. "Seems like you've assaulted and made threats against Mr. Easton, one of the esteemed residents of my town."

Merritt felt Jack go still at those words.

Danna had claimed him as a resident of Calvin.

"It's time for you to leave," Danna said evenly. "Don't ever come back."

Jack stood on the boardwalk with the woman he loved beside him, cold air cutting through his shirt. They remained side by side and watched Danna and her men escort Morris away.

. . . one of the esteemed residents of my town.

A curious numbness had stolen over him at her words.

Now, Merritt's hand slipped into his, the warmth of her palm welcome as she linked their fingers together.

And everything rushed back. He felt all of it. The overwhelming relief that Morris hadn't hurt her. That Jack had arrived in time. That Nick had been present and that Danna had come . . .

"How'd you get inside?" Merritt asked quietly.

He could hear the echo of muffled voices inside, knew that she must need to return to the dance hall. People were waiting on her.

But he couldn't make himself let go of her hand so she could walk back inside.

"I met up with your cousin on my way into town."

"Which one?"

"Nick. We were heading for the dance hall when we saw Morris burst inside. Nick knew about the window, and I didn't particularly want to get shot."

She tipped her head to the side, and he could only let himself glance at her for a beat. There was too much pain and joy wrapped up in this moment, and nothing was resolved between them.

"The second-story window," she said.

"That's the one. The kids were up there—it took two of the boys to pry it open. Once I made it through the window, they told me you'd sent them."

"Surely you didn't scale the side of a building."

He chuckled a little. "It's been years since I've climbed a tree, so no. But Nick has his horse trained incredibly well. He put the horse up on the boardwalk, and from the saddle, Nick was able to boost me to the windowsill."

There'd been a terrifying moment when Jack had been hanging by his fingertips from the sill as Nick's horse clomped out from underneath him. He'd been afraid he wouldn't have the strength to pull himself up into the window, but he'd heard a scream from inside, and the next thing he knew, his shoulders were in the window, and Paul was gripping the back of his trousers to pull him all the way inside.

He'd gotten lucky. He knew it.

"I'm sorry he came after you"—she'd never know how sorry—"and interrupted your special night." He'd seen the raw fear in her expression as he'd walked down the stairs.

Her hand squeezed his. "I can't believe you came back—"

"Miss Harding."

Merritt blinked, accepting the interruption as three pairs of footsteps clomped on the boardwalk.

It was her school board members. In the dim light thrown by the open doors, Jack saw the smirk worn by Polk.

"I am sorry to say that what happened tonight has shown us clearly that you are no longer fit to be the schoolteacher of the Calvin school."

"That's not what we discussed," said Mr. Goodall, a man with a gray mustache and bowler hat. From his position next to Mr. Polk, his gaze flicked to Jack.

If anything, Polk's smile grew wider. "When we discussed Miss Harding's tenure earlier today, we had only taken into account her dallying with a known gambler of ill repute. But it's clear by what happened tonight that her actions have endangered the children in her care—"

Jack let go of Merritt's hand to take a step in the man's direction. "Merritt used her quick thinking to get those kids out of harm's way."

Polk's lip curled. "They wouldn't have been in harm's way if not for her connection with you and your *acquaintances*."

"You can't take away Miss Harding's job," Jack insisted, though he knew it was well within their rights.

Merritt came beside him, her hand snaking around his arm. "It's all right," she said softly.

"It's not all right." His sense of justice was riled, and he felt righteous anger pouring through him.

"It's not going to matter in the end." Polk glanced at the other two board members. "Unfortunately, I've been in talks with Ernie Duff from the land office, and he's combed through the record books. There's no official record that the land where the school building was constructed was ever purchased by the township. In fact, only yesterday, Burns filed a deed for that tract of land."

Merritt went still beside him. Jack's chest expanded, but before he could speak, Mr. Goodall said, "What do you mean, no record of the original deed?"

"Just what I said." There was such a slimy tone in Polk's voice that Jack wanted to slug him. "The title for that piece of land has been bought and paid for. When I asked Duff where we might rebuild the school, he told me that every parcel in the township was spoken for, unless we can have the town council expand the borders of our town."

"The school is centrally located," Merritt said. "Easy for any child living nearby to walk to. If it's relocated outside of town, some children won't be able to attend."

"That's too bad," Polk said. "*If* the school is rebuilt before the spring semester ends. You know how the town council can be so terribly slow about passing legislation."

Another pair of boots hit the boardwalk, and Jack was deeply relieved as Nick headed their direction.

"Gentlemen." Nick shook hands with all three school board members. If Jack wasn't mistaken, he squeezed Polk's for a prolonged moment. The other man flexed his hand at his side, as if Nick's handshake had hurt, and Jack felt an inordinate amount of happiness in that.

"I couldn't help but overhear your lively discussion." Nick pulled a sheaf of papers from an inside coat pocket.

"I just came in on the train from Cheyenne, where I had a visit with the state superintendent. Mr. Beauchamp has been remitting a report on our county school each year. But did you know that his predecessor wrote terribly detailed reports? The superintendent sent me with a handwritten copy of this one." Nick held out a paper to Mr. Goodall, who took it. "As you can see there, it shows the detail of the land parcel where the school was, before it burned."

"Regardless, if the school was occupying the land illegally—"

Nick interrupted Polk. "It was legal, even if the records have been lost. There are six years of reports just like that one. The state office also told me about state legislation passed just last year reserving a parcel of land in each township specifically for a school. The superintendent was going to wire Mr. Duff over at the land office so he'd have an official reminder."

Mr. Goodall stared at the paper with a frown. "The sale to Mr. Burns can be reversed. It's clear he was trying to take advantage of the situation."

Polk started to argue, and Mr. Beauchamp joined the conversation.

"Nick!" Merritt moved past Jack and threw her arms around her cousin. Over her head, Nick's stare bored into Jack.

Thank you, Jack mouthed.

Take care of her, Nick replied in kind.

Mr. Goodall looked to Merritt. "You go on back inside, Miss Harding. Your students are waiting for you. You've done good work tonight, this week. You don't need to worry about your job."

Jack felt a sense of satisfaction as her face glowed under the praise.

"But—" Polk spluttered.

Goodall clapped a hand on the other man's back. "I think we're finished here."

Beauchamp had already started down the street. "Won't hurt to go and visit Mr. Duff right now."

The night went quiet as the three men continued arguing on their way down the street. From inside, voices of children and parents were muffled.

Jack stood shivering on the edge of the boardwalk. He felt a sense of satisfaction. He'd accomplished what he'd come back to do.

. . . one of the esteemed residents of my town.

Was there a chance he could stay?

Merritt was concentrating on her cousin. "Nick, come in and watch."

But as Jack watched, some pain passed over Nick's expression. "Not tonight."

Merritt looked sympathetic and understanding. "Perhaps next time."

Jack had figured a man who'd once wanted to be a teacher might like to come in and watch the children perform. But Nick shook his head again, sharing secrets with Merritt that Jack didn't know.

Nick left and then it was only Jack and Merritt standing in the quiet night. She was facing away from him as she reached out and pulled open the door, letting light spill out. He couldn't help remembering the way she'd cried just after the last time he'd seen her. Maybe he should go . . .

Except she turned and looked at him, the glowing lamplight gilding every side of her like she was some kind of angel. His heart twisted.

She motioned him forward, and he sent another prayer upward to the God he'd only begun to introduce himself to, that his luck wouldn't run out yet.

She handed him his coat, and he hung back at the rear of the room as she moved through the throngs of parents and kids. Nobody seemed terribly traumatized, everyone chatting like tonight was any other night.

Merritt stood on the stage and asked everyone to sit down, asked the kids to start all over again.

When he thought she would've stayed up front to keep things running, she leaned over to whisper to one of the bigger girls and then skirted the crowd that was watching the children with rapt attention to stand next to him along the back wall.

"You left," she whispered without taking her eyes off the action on the makeshift stage.

"I did." He'd only made it as far as the next town over. Between Cecil on the train and his own conscience, he hadn't needed much convincing. "I didn't get far. I realized I'd left behind everything that mattered."

He heard the catch in her breath but also saw one of the men in the back row craning his neck to catch sight of the two of them before he turned back around.

So Jack didn't take her hand or turn toward her, even though everything inside him longed to take her in his arms. "I'm sorry," he said. "Sorry for lying to you, sorry for putting you in danger. But I'm not sorry we met—"

"Me neither."

Her whispered words sank into him, to the deepest part of his heart, and for the first time since he'd left her in the preacher's parlor, he felt a beat of hope, like the first crocus leaf popping out of the snow in spring.

He couldn't stop himself this time, turned toward her, though he was careful to hide the way his hand closed over hers with the shift of his body.

Her eyes were luminous as she gave him her entire focus.

"I know we haven't known each other long and that you'll want to know a lot more about me before you can say the same, but"—he swallowed hard—"I'm falling in love with you."

"Oh, Jack." She was looking at him in such a way that he couldn't help inching closer. "I know enough about your honorable intentions that I'm falling too."

Her words settled inside him, breaking him apart and putting him back together. He felt like a brand-new man, at once effervescent with joy and grounded like a foundation stone in a house.

She reached for him and he felt a rush of relief as he stepped closer, as her arms wound around his waist, as his hands rested behind her back. She was in his arms again, and it was heaven.

But he didn't tip his head to take the kiss he wanted, even though her chin was tilted in delightful invitation.

And then she asked. "Aren't you going to kiss me? A declaration like that seems as if it should be punctuated with a kiss."

There was his independent schoolmarm. Not afraid to ask for what she wanted.

"There's a whole lotta kids up on that stage," he whispered. "What're the chances they'll ignore us?"

"Very low." But she was grinning up at him. "Lower than finding an ace on your first draw from the deck. But you should probably do it anyway."

He bent his head and brushed his lips across hers. Joy rose up inside him, full and resonant.

She returned his feelings. She was in his arms.

"Stay in Calvin," she whispered when they parted. "Build a home here—with me."

When his eyes started to smart, she pressed her cheek to his shoulder.

That must've been the moment the pageant ended, because there was a thunderous roar of applause and stomping feet.

But he was in his own little world, holding the most precious piece of his heart.

Fourteen

K NOCK, KNOCK.
Another one?
Jack registered the knock on Merritt's front door from where he squatted in front of the open door of her kitchen stove. He could still hear Merritt in her bedroom, rustling around behind a closed door, so he went into her parlor to answer.

"Happy Christmas!" Both Paul and Daniel stood on the stoop, wearing almost identical smiles.

"Hello," Jack said, even though tomorrow was Christmas. Word seemed to have gotten out in town that the beloved schoolmarm was traveling to see her cousins.

"We brought Miss Harding a Christmas gift," Daniel said. He did, in fact, hold a cloth-wrapped bundle in his hands.

"I can see that." It'd only been two days since the pageant, since Morris had been sent away, and Jack still found himself scanning the quiet street for any sign of danger. It was empty, only the rented horse and carriage waiting for Merritt and Jack, same as it had been for the past half hour. The horse had a bough of green holly with red berries tied to its harness.

Jack stepped aside so they could enter.

He heard Merritt's bedroom door open, and his heart sped up when she entered the room, a carpetbag in her hands, her face turned back to the bedroom, and her lower lip between her teeth in distraction. He'd been in her presence all morning, but she still affected him. He hoped it would always be like that.

She blinked when she registered her guests. "Hello, boys! Oh, please tell me that's one of your mother's famous fruitcakes, Daniel."

The boy pulled back the cloth to show that it was.

Paul pushed his hands in his pockets as Merritt exclaimed over the treat, taking it to the table where it joined a ham, a book of poetry, and some crudely knitted mittens. Her students had been stopping by all morning.

Daniel glanced at the other boy. "Paul's got a gift too."

Jack didn't see one anywhere. Was this another of the boys' competitions? Another way for them to harass each other?

"Mine's not . . . something you can see," Paul said awkwardly. His chin jutted up stubbornly. "I decided to apply for some medical schools, like you said."

Merritt squealed as if she'd received the best news ever. She came to throw one arm around the boy's shoulder. "I'm thrilled to hear that."

Paul looked a little chagrined. "I'll need your help to find some of those scalla—skrulla—"

"Scholarships. Of course."

Daniel cocked his head. "Y'all are gonna get married, aren't ya?"

Jack's heart kicked and his mouth went dry. What an impertinent question! He'd been careful not to bring it up these past two days since he'd come back to Calvin. It was too soon, and he knew it.

But apparently the boy had no compunction asking about it.

Merritt glanced at Jack, and when he saw the quiet, steady happiness in her expression, the roaring of his pulse in his ears receded.

"Someday," she told Daniel—and Paul, who'd perked up for the answer too.

Someday.

Same way it did in unexpected moments every day, the love filling up his heart overflowed. Merritt was something special. And by some miracle of God's grace, she was his.

Daniel moved toward the door. "I might wanna be a doctor too. Gotta talk to my folks. Come on, Paul. Seems Mr. Jack's got a Christmas trip planned."

The boys trooped out the door with grins and waves.

"They seem to have worked things out between them," he murmured as Merritt closed the door and turned to face the room, beaming quietly.

"Partly because of you," she said. "They worked together to keep the children out of harm's way during the scuffle."

He shook his head. If she wanted to think something

good had happened because of Morris's threat, that was her business.

"Are you ready for your Christmas trip?" she asked with a laugh.

"It's not my trip," he protested, but he couldn't keep up the facade of being perturbed when she giggled.

"Never say you're nervous," she teased him.

"I'm terrified."

Now she burst out in peals of laughter. "Tillie will be devastated if we don't go."

"I know."

He'd known that things would be different between them now. There was no pretend engagement, only a commitment to see where things led. Which was why he'd been shocked when she'd asked him to come with her to spend Christmas with the McGraws on the family homestead, a half-day's ride out of town.

Merritt turned toward the kitchen.

"I'll get that brick I've got warming in the coals," he said, trailing her.

"All right. There's one more thing . . . "

But she'd stopped short, right where he'd hung his coat over the back of one of her kitchen chairs. Bent down to pick up something off the floor. "What's this?"

He recognized the folded piece of paper even as she glanced curiously at him.

He stepped toward her, stretched out his hand. "It's nothing—"

But she was already unfolding the paper, her eyes scanning its contents.

He turned away, let his hand come up to run through the hair at the back of his neck. Let out a gusty sigh.

Pride had kept him hoping she'd never see that piece of paper. Why had he put it in his coat pocket? It must've fallen out when he'd taken off his coat earlier. He'd been too careless.

"Jack?"

He had no choice but to turn at the soft query in her voice. She had the note open but was looking right at him.

He knew what she'd seen on that paper. The crudely drawn letters that Jack had tried to assemble into words. He'd used a dime-store novel he'd found beneath the bed in his room at the boardinghouse to help him with the spelling.

He'd given up halfway down the page when he'd realized the words that slanted across the paper, falling off their lines, looked more like something a first-year student would write than anything else.

He cleared his throat because Merritt was waiting on an answer. "You started liking your John because of his letters. I thought I might write a letter for you, but—"

Here he had to swallow hard as she glanced back down at the paper in her hands. It was silly, but he felt a flush climbing into his neck. "What little schooling I had was in broken snatches. I couldn't finish."

Her eyes were soft as she stepped forward and came easily into his arms. There was a relief in burying his face in her hair, even as she spoke into his shoulder.

"He was never *my* John. Not in the way you're mine."

The emotion that was never far away swirled inside him in a dizzying spiral, and he held her that much more tightly.

"We should get in the buggy and go," he murmured into her hair. Because the longer he kept holding her like this, the less he wanted to let her go.

"Not yet, I want to—"

But another sharp knock on the door interrupted her.

She wrinkled her nose as she pushed away from him. "We'll never leave if students keep stopping by."

But there was clear affection in her voice, and he knew how each student who delivered a gift made her feel valued and loved. As she deserved.

But it wasn't a student in the doorway when she opened it this time. It was the marshal. She had the baby in the crook of her arm, and a little girl with pigtails, wearing a coat that almost swallowed her, peeked past her thigh.

Jack's stomach did the same funny little shiver it always did when he was faced with a lawman, but he also had the echo of her words from the other night in his memory.

"Merry Christmas." Danna hugged Merritt and stepped inside. "I'm glad I caught you before you left."

"If you need a last-minute gift for Chas, I'm afraid I can't help you."

Danna pulled a face at her friend. "Actually, I need to talk to Jack."

She did?

For a moment, his thoughts tunneled into a negative spiral. She'd changed her mind about him. He wasn't welcome here.

He steadied himself on an inhale as Merritt came to

stand beside him and slipped her hand into his. It was a reminder that whatever happened, he wasn't alone. Not anymore.

Danna appraised him steadily. "Wanted to let you know that Morris is long gone. I escorted him onto the train myself. My deputies will keep an eye out if he tries to return."

The last bit of tension from that situation dissolved like snow on a hot stove.

But the marshal wasn't finished. "I've spoken to several folks about what happened in the dance hall two nights ago."

That didn't sound promising. Jack's heart sank.

"Every single one of them mentioned how calm you were under pressure."

Her words had him blinking in surprise. He hadn't felt calm, not with Merritt within arm's reach of that thug, Morris.

"And I've been told you're looking for work." That matter was a bit more prickly. He felt Merritt tense at his side and realized she must've been the one to share that with the marshal. He couldn't fault her; he knew the two women were friends. It was his own pride that was pricked, knowing he didn't have many skills that would translate well to a life in this small town.

"I could use another deputy," the marshal said. "Some of the homesteaders are getting into disputes with the ranchers who have bigger spreads. Burns's attempt at getting his hands on that land was shut down, but he still plans to build another saloon. That'll mean more drunken cowboys. I think you'd be a good fit for the office."

He must've looked as bowled over as he felt, because Merritt hid a laugh behind her hand.

"You want *me* . . . to be a deputy?"

Danna looked as serious as he'd ever seen her, even though her hand rested on the little girl's head. "I'd be proud to have you working at my side. You've made a difference for a lot of people without taking any recognition for it. Maybe it's time you pin on a badge."

He promised to think about it, and she took her leave after a few words to Merritt.

He couldn't believe it. The marshal wanted him for a deputy? The job would give him the financial security he wanted to provide for Merritt and their future family. It would be a tie to Calvin, to the community here.

It felt too good to be true. Like God had dropped the biggest pot imaginable right into Jack's lap.

Merritt gave Jack a moment as he murmured something about getting the brick out of the stove. He seemed to need the time to get his head on straight.

It was the least she could give him. He'd seemed so surprised by Danna's offer. And she'd felt the relief shudder through him when she'd held him close after she'd seen that half-page letter he'd written. Like he was still waiting for the other shoe to drop. Waiting for Merritt—or the town—to find him unworthy.

Merritt said a little prayer for him as she went to her room and grabbed Jack's hat off the end of her bed.

She met him in the parlor. He'd donned his coat and was

coming in from where he must've put his warming brick in the carriage.

"Maybe I can give this to you without interruption this time," she said.

She went to him, extending the hat she'd gifted him once before. "It was yours, always meant to be yours."

His nostrils flared slightly as he took the upturned hat from her, then he frowned as he realized there was something inside the crown.

He reached inside and plucked out the black leather gloves she'd tucked inside. "Merritt . . . "

"I wanted to," she said. She felt the echo of what he'd told her once before as his face held an almost disbelieving expression—a hint of the boy who'd never been given a Christmas gift before. It wasn't right, and she couldn't make it right, but she'd wanted to give him more than just the hat.

"Thank you." His voice was rough, and he cleared his throat and slipped the gloves into his coat pocket, pulled the hat into place on his head. He went to the sofa, where a brown-wrapped package rested. Had she walked right by it without seeing it?

"This is for you. Merry Christmas."

He'd been open with her about his lack of funds—and that he didn't want to visit a poker table again, not when he needed to clean up his reputation.

"You shouldn't have," she murmured. But she reached for the twine holding the paper closed anyway.

"Albert Hyer let me put it on credit. He said he knew I was good for it." Merritt was concentrating on folding back the paper, but she still heard the note of incredulousness in Jack's voice. Another sign of the folks in town accepting him.

The paper fell away and revealed a lovely lace shawl.

"Oh, Jack." Her eyes smarted, filling with tears. It was beautiful.

"Mrs. Quinn told me you'd bid on one like it at the auction until the price got too high. If you don't like it—"

"I love it." She held it to her chest and looked up at him, letting him see everything she felt. It had been a long time since she'd received a gift like this. Impractical, beautiful, something given to her simply because she liked it.

Jack had given her that. Brought beauty and love back into her life.

"I can't wait for the weather to warm. I'll wear it every Sunday morning to church."

A hint of relief passed through his eyes. "I'm glad."

He tugged her toward the door. "We should go. Before someone else knocks on that door."

She secured her new gift safely in the bureau in her bedroom and found Jack had already lifted her carpetbag. "I'm ready."

Outside, he helped her into the carriage and took his time tucking the lap blanket around her feet, making sure the brick he'd wrapped in cloth was right beneath her to keep her warm.

And then the conveyance jostled as he climbed up beside her. His shoulder nudged hers as he settled in the seat. She tucked the lap blanket over his legs, and he clasped her hand briefly in thanks before he tapped the reins and the horse Merritt had rented from the livery sprang into a walk.

She tucked her arm through his, felt the cold winter sunshine on her cheeks.

"If you've never received a Christmas gift," she wondered aloud, "what about for your birthday?"

"I don't know it," he said. "The orphanage didn't exactly celebrate and neither did the Farr family."

There was no trace of bitterness in his voice. Only a hint of sadness, maybe for the boy he'd been.

"We could celebrate together," she said. "My birthday is in May."

He rested his cheek on the top of her head, his hat casting a shadow on her face. "I'd like that."

Mr. and Mrs. Hyer were walking down the boardwalk, arm in arm, and Twila looked up and saw Merritt and Jack in the buggy. She waved happily.

Merritt found herself beaming back. All those months ago, she'd attended their wedding and felt such a deep emptiness, thought of everything that her life was missing.

They traveled out of town, and the landscape opened up in front of them, only a dusting of snow hanging on from days ago, the mountains in the far distance purple against the horizon.

Jack had arrived in town in such an unexpected way. She'd expected John, and God had brought Jack into her life. A man she'd never have chosen, wouldn't have gotten to know well enough to discover his compassionate heart, the boy who had overcome a terrible upbringing to become a man of honor.

He shifted the reins to his left hand and moved his right

so that their hands were linked together. He'd worn the new gloves and it made her smile.

She had the family she'd always wanted in Jack. And if God blessed them in the future, a house full of children.

She'd been given everything she'd dreamed of.

"I love you," she whispered.

She felt him stiffen for a moment, then relax. Would he ever stop expecting the worst? She didn't know. But the simple joy in his face every time he heard words like the ones she'd just said were enough for now.

He pressed a kiss on top of her head. "I love you too. I'll love you even more if you protect me from your cousins."

A smile stretched across her lips. "I think you've already won Nick to your side." And Drew, too, if he'd sent the youngest brother on such an errand to help Merritt and the schoolhouse.

"Nick isn't the scary one. Have you seen Drew's glower?"

She turned her smile into his shoulder but couldn't resist teasing him once more. "You haven't met Isaac yet."

He groaned and she laughed. She couldn't imagine a better Christmas than one spent with family and the man she loved.

"You've got your whole life ahead of you to win them over," she said. "Just be yourself. I fell in love with you. They will too."

His hand squeezed hers. "I'll try."

She couldn't ask for anything more.

Bonus Epilogue

Are you a member of my our releases newsletter? You can receive a special gift, available only to newsletters subscribers. This Bonus Epilogue to *A Convenient Heart* will not be released on any retailer platform—it's only available to newsletter subscribers.

Find out what happens next with Merrit and Jack. Scan this QR code to subscribe and get your free gift. Unsubscribe at any time.

Acknowledgments

With thanks to Susie and the Sunrise team for this fun experience and a chance to work together.

About the Author

USA Today bestselling author **Lacy Williams** is devoted to bringing her readers heartwarming love stories about cowboys and the women that tame them. She is the author of over fifty-five books, including the acclaimed Wind River Hearts and Sutter's Hollow series. Her books have been nominated for the RT Book Reviews' Seal of Excellence as well as finaled in RT's Reviewers' Choice Awards. She has been a puppy parent almost her whole life and often writes with one of her dogs snuggled in her lap. She is a mom of four and spends her non-writing time buried under piles of laundry and dishes.

Learn more at lacywilliams.net.

DON'T MISS THE NEXT ROMANTIC
WIND RIVER MAIL-ORDER BRIDE NOVEL
BY LACY WILLIAMS AND MARTHA HUTCHENS.

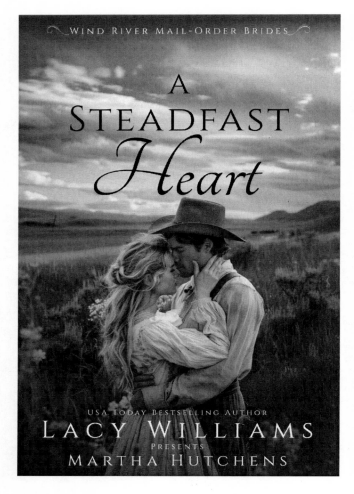

A SINGLE DAD, A MAIL-ORDER BRIDE,
BUT IS KAITLYN MONTGOMERY READY FOR
THIS READY-MADE FAMILY?

When his family legacy is on the line, rancher Drew McGraw becomes desperate for someone to tame and tutor his three children. Desperate enough to seek a mail-order bride. But when the wrong woman arrives on his doorstep, Drew balks.

Heiress Kaitlyn Montgomery runs straight from the scandal chasing her toward a fresh start on a secluded ranch. She strikes a bargain with Drew—a marriage convenient for both of them. One with an end date.

But the more Kaitlyn adapts to ranch life and forms a bond with Drew's children and their enigmatic father, she realizes that this ranch is where she is meant to be. And then her past catches up with her...

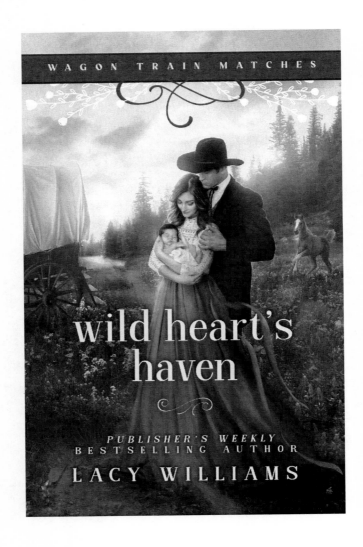

One

HOLLIS WILL BE OUT WITH THE LEAD wagon."

The woman walking beside Owen Mason barely acknowledged his words, and he felt a stirring of irritation. He worked to quash it.

Rachel Duncan might be the stubbornest, most independent woman he'd ever met. Her dark honey-colored hair and blue-eyed gaze might've been pleasing if not for the irritation he felt every time she opened her mouth to speak. She bothered him like a burr under his saddle. Made his skin itch like it was crawling with ants.

And Owen had promised to marry her.

That's why he needed Hollis Tremblay, the wagon master of their company. To perform the ceremony.

The sun had been up for almost an hour. The wagon train camp along the Platte River was bustling with activity as every traveler, even the children, helped prepare to pull out for the day. Their caravan had been on the trail West to Oregon for weeks now, and the company knew the routine for readying for a day of travel.

Owen needed to find Hollis, fast. The bugle—the signal to pull out—was about to blow. He skirted a girl no older than ten who was trying to shoo two chickens into a large wicker basket.

"Sorry."

He glanced over his shoulder at Rachel's murmured apology to see chickens scattering in opposite directions. The girl's basket was on the ground, and she was glaring at Rachel.

Rachel had one hand pressed against her opposite elbow, as if she'd bumped it.

Probably bumped it on the little girl. Had she run into her?

It was plausible, given Rachel's condition. The woman was due to give birth in the next few weeks. He doubted she could see her feet when she was standing up, and she was clumsy. He'd seen it himself, watched her knock over a pail of fresh water from the creek because she hadn't seen it on the ground in front of her.

She caught his gaze and her lips pinched. She always wore a sour expression when she looked at him.

Guilt surged. Maybe he deserved it.

The wound in his arm—a thin line between a scrape and a cut on the outside of his biceps—pulsed in time with his heartbeat. He slowed his stride slightly so she could keep up, but the urgency inside him didn't go away.

He wanted to get this over with.

Owen came across Leo Spencer and his wife, near their wagon. His older half-brother had fallen in love on the earliest days of the trail and married Evangeline.

Their campsite was packed up. The fire had been stamped out. Evangeline's young sister, Sara, played on the wagon seat, away from the dangerous hooves of the oxen already in their traces.

Judging by the way he and Evangeline stood so close against the wagon, Leo must've thought everyone else around was too busy to pay attention. Leo was the same height as Owen, and sometimes looking at him was akin to looking at Owen's own reflection. They both resembled their late father with his dark hair and eyes.

Leo had his arms around Evangeline's waist, and as Owen watched, he raised one hand to brush against Evangeline's cheek. The clear affection and love in Leo's expression twisted Owen up inside.

It didn't matter. Owen had no use for a love match. Or any match at all. He was only going through with this because it was the right thing to do.

Leo must've caught sight of Owen striding through camp because he glanced over his shoulder and then dropped his hand, though he didn't look embarrassed to be caught snuggling his wife.

"You seen Hollis?" Owen called.

Leo shook his head negatively. "You seen Coop?"

"I haven't," Owen responded. Coop was Leo's younger brother, no relation to Owen.

Owen halted abruptly and Rachel almost plowed into him. He stopped her forward momentum with a hand on her elbow, though he quickly dropped it, shaking out the ache from his wound.

She gave him a squinty-eyed glare when he turned to her. "Why don't you wait here? I'll go fetch Hollis."

"It will be quicker if I go with you."

He couldn't recall a conversation with Rachel where she hadn't argued with him. Irritation stung like nettles all over his skin. He rolled his shoulders to try and get rid of the feeling. The pulse of pain in his arm grew more intense and then faded.

"We'll need witnesses anyway." He was aware of Leo's sharp sideways glance, but continued, "Just stay put."

He heard the gurgle of her stomach. His eyebrows raised of their own volition. "Have you eaten anything today?"

Her frown was answer enough.

He looked past Rachel to Evangeline, who was speaking to Sara. He called out, "Can you help Rachel scrounge up some breakfast?"

Evangeline murmured a quiet, "Of course," but he was already striding away, intent on finding Hollis so he could get this over with.

Leo jogged to fall into step beside Owen.

"What do you need Hollis for? And witnesses?"

Owen wasn't used to being on the other end of Leo's big brother inquisition. Leo was three years older, which made Owen the same age as Collin and Coop, Leo's twin brothers from another father.

Owen had grown up in California, never knowing he had a brother and sister until his father had been dying of consumption and revealed it on his deathbed. Owen had made a difficult decision to go back east to try and find his siblings.

He was used to being the older brother. The problem solver. The responsible one.

And Owen had found them in a spot of trouble.

Leo hadn't wanted anything to do with Owen those

first weeks. Owen thought things had smoothed over between them, but that muscle ticking in his brother's jaw maybe meant things were still a little tumultuous.

"What do you need Hollis for?" Leo repeated.

Owen might as well tell him. It wasn't easy to keep secrets on the trail. With only a flimsy piece of canvas between you and your next neighbor, it was far too easy to overhear conversations.

"I'm marrying Rachel."

Leo snorted, but then grew serious when he realized Owen wasn't joking. "You can't marry her. You hate each other."

"I don't hate her." He couldn't say she felt the same. Not for certain.

At their first meeting, she had been pointing a gun—empty at the time, but he hadn't known that—at Owen's younger brother, August. So Owen had tackled her to the ground. She'd been terrified, hiding from the men who had massacred her wagon train, and it had been dark. He hadn't realized until everything was over that she was a she, and that she was pregnant.

Even if she had forgiven him for that, there was other bad blood between them.

"Maybe you don't hate her, but you sure don't like her."

Leo was right. Owen and Rachel couldn't seem to help arguing at every turn.

He sighed and stopped, turning to face his brother.

"It's my fault Daniel got himself killed." It was the first time he'd said the words out loud. But not the first time he'd thought them.

Leo's frown deepened. "How d'you figure? Daniel

was a bully who tried to steal a horse, then tried to steal a wagon."

Rachel's brother had been shot in the middle of a gunfight when Owen and Leo and the others from their company had been defending against an outlaw band who'd tried to murder them and steal their supplies and animals—the same outlaw band that had killed Rachel's other family.

"I should've tied him hand and foot," Owen said.

Or had one of the younger men hold him at gunpoint. Maybe given him a horse and sent him on his way.

Any choice but the one Owen had made could've resulted in a different outcome.

The other men from the wagon train—including the one Daniel had attempted to steal a horse from—had wanted him hanged. Owen had thought he was sparing Daniel's life to bring him to the fort.

Daniel hadn't survived that long.

And Owen might never forget the keening wail Rachel had let out when she'd seen her brother's lifeless body.

Leo's voice shook him out of that terrible memory. "Guilt isn't something to build a marriage on."

Leo was as serious as Owen had ever seen him. His voice held an edge Owen hadn't heard in weeks.

But at Leo's words, Owen felt his shoulders relax. "It's only until we reach Oregon," he told his brother. "Then we'll have it annulled."

Leo scowled.

"What?" Owen was honestly confused at his brother's response.

"You'd marry her and walk away?" Now Leo sounded offended. And as far as Owen was concerned, this wasn't his business.

"This isn't a love match." Owen couldn't help it. He bristled at Leo's commanding tone. "It's an agreement between the two of us."

Leo sneered. "It sounds like something our pa would've done. He left one wife behind easily enough."

Was that what Leo was worried about? "I won't leave her penniless."

Leo shook his head. "I thought you were different. But there's a lot of Pa in you, isn't there?"

Owen took offense to that. "Our father was an up-standing man. A man of honor—"

"Except when he walked away from his family."

Leo's words felt like a slap. He wasn't done yet. "And you're gonna do the same. There's nothing honorable in what you're doing."

Leo whirled on his heel and stomped off, leaving Owen fuming. He strode through a couple of parked wagons, grateful there weren't any travelers nearby to have heard the words exchanged by the brothers.

Leo had no right to talk to him that way. Leo didn't understand.

Owen was trying to do right by Rachel. Maybe it wasn't entirely his fault that her brother was a no-account thief who didn't mind bullying his pregnant sister when he got drunk. But he'd been a part of what had happened.

Marrying Rachel meant she'd have the protection of his name until they reached Oregon. That was enough to settle the debt between them.

It didn't matter whether Leo liked it or not. Owen

had lived his entire life, until the past nine months, believing he was the older brother. He'd been raised to do the right thing. Take responsibility. He took care of his own. He was a man.

And he was man enough to make this decision.

Available now!

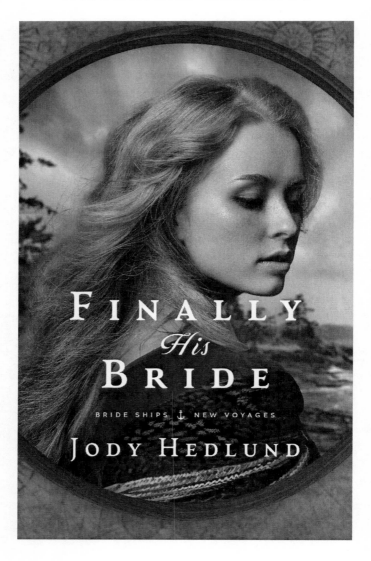

One

Manchester, England
September 1862

YOU HAVE TO GO, WILLOW." DAD'S voice was low and pleading. "We wouldn't ask this of you if there was any other way."

Willow Rhodes tried to draw a breath into her rapidly constricting airways. She sat with her head bent and elbows on her knees, but instead of the position helping her, she only seemed to gasp more.

Her mum rubbed her back. "It really is the best plan, poppet."

"The only plan," Dad mumbled, drumming his thumbs on the table.

On the bench across from him, Willow pushed down the rising panic. As the oldest of five daughters, she knew she had to be the one to save her family from their desperate situation, but this . . .? Go on a bride ship halfway around the world? She couldn't.

"I'll do it." Briar spoke up from the edge of the bed where she, Fern, and Clover were perched, watching the unfolding drama in their one-room flat, their pretty heart-shaped faces, dainty chins, and high cheekbones characteristic of all the Rhodes women. Briar shared brown eyes and darker auburn hair with Fern, taking after their dad. But Willow and Clover had the same blue eyes and reddish-blond hair as their mum . . . and so did Sage.

Smart, capable, and pretty Sage. Mum and Dad would never consider sending their most responsible daughter away. Besides, Sage would be married soon enough to David who worked in the catgut factory and hadn't been affected by the lack of cotton that had closed the mills.

Briar stood, her wooden clogs slapping against the thin floorboards, her faded skirt having been washed so many times it was as gray as the Manchester sky. "If Willow doesn't want to go, then I'll happily take her place."

"You're too young, luv." Dad ran his fingers through what was left of his thin hair. His shoulders were bony, and his clothes hung on his frame too loosely. Long gone was the robust, sun-tanned, muscular man who'd once spent his every waking moment farming.

"I'm almost seventeen." Briar stood as tall as she could, but even holding her head high, she was still shorter than Fern and Clover. "I heard Miss Rye isn't particular about the age."

"I'm particular." Dad slid back from the table, but before he could stand, he burst into a cough—a deep, hacking cough that had grown worse over the summer and didn't appear to be getting any better with the coming of the cooler autumn days.

No one would say the words white lung disease. But everyone knew that's what afflicted him after fifteen years of toiling in the cotton mill as a mule spinner, making sure the threads didn't get caught or tangled as they wound around the many spools. He'd inhaled the humid air full of cotton dust for so many years, his lungs were irreparably damaged.

Willow's own breathing problems were probably related to the mill too. She hadn't worked there as long as her dad, but laboring ten-hour days for the past four years had taken a toll. It was one more reason her parents wanted her to leave Manchester, so that when the mills finally reopened, she wouldn't be tempted to return and ruin her lungs even further.

With the start of war in America, no one knew when cotton imports from the southern states would resume. Most speculated that the conflict wouldn't last long, maybe would be over in a few months by the end of 1862 or early next year. Until then, without cotton, hundreds of thousands of mill workers in Manchester and Lancashire—Cottonopolis—were unemployed.

Willow's stomach grumbled, and she fisted her hand against it, trying to ease the ache. But the ache hadn't gone away over the past couple of months since they'd had no income and no way to purchase food. They'd had to rely upon the charity groups who'd heard about the widespread unemployment and had come to Manchester to assist. As well-meaning as the charities were—and she was grateful for them—the lines were long and the portions were never enough to truly satisfy.

"Think about it, poppet." Mum rubbed her back

again and stared unseeingly out the lone high window of their ground-floor flat that showed only the narrow street that ran in front of their rowhouse. "You'll get out of the city, get the fresh air you need, and have plenty of food."

Her mum was probably envisioning the borough where she'd grown up, the wide-open fields of rural Lancashire that they'd called home before being forced off the land through the enclosure laws.

Mum's face, like Dad's, had grown pale and thin over the years of living in the dirty, overcrowded city where the coal smoke blasting from hundreds of factories cast a haze over the sky so that the sun was a rare sight.

Mum had tried to bring the sunshine into their home by painting their walls and furniture yellow. The chairs, the table, the sideboard, the chest of drawers, and even the trunk at the end of the bed were all yellow. She'd painted every glass jar and bottle she could find yellow and had filled them with wildflowers she'd picked and dried whenever they ventured out of the city on holiday.

Willow's gaze touched on each bright spot in the home. The yellow had faded regardless of her mum's efforts to wash and repaint and keep the color bright. Even pale, the yellow amidst the drabness of everything else had always reminded Willow of how hard her parents had worked to love her and her sisters and give them a good life in spite of the hardships.

Was it her turn to do something good for them . . . no matter how difficult it would be? And it would be difficult. New tasks always took her longer than usual to understand. It had been the same with reading at the

Ragged School. She'd mixed up letters and words and had to reread the passage a couple of times before she comprehended it.

Dad finished coughing and cleared his throat. "Miss Rye says that as a domestic in the colony, you'll have a free place to stay. In no time, you'll have enough to cover the passage for your sisters. Yeah?"

"And you and Mum."

With drawn brows, Dad shared a glance with Mum.

"Send both Willow and me," Briar insisted. "We'll be able to save for everyone."

Dad shook his head, his eyes growing sad. "Miss Rye filled up the last of the spots."

"Then let me go since Willow isn't sure—"

"No, Briar." Willow stood. "If anyone is leaving home, it'll be me."

Her dad's pallid face was turning splotchy red, likely in an effort to keep from hacking again. "I'd be the one to go ahead if I could."

Even in the dimness of the evening, Willow had no trouble viewing her dear family. They meant everything to her. And if her going would help them, how could she reject the plan? "Where is the ship heading?"

"Vancouver Island." Her dad spoke with forced enthusiasm. "I'm told it's a twin sister to merry old England, that everyone who lives there feels right at home."

"Right at home? Where?" The door opened, and Caleb stepped inside. With the brim of his flat cap pulled low over his short dark hair, his face was shadowed, giving his scruffy facial hair a darker than usual tint. He carried his wool coat slung over his broad shoulders, revealing his suspenders and shirt stretched taut over his muscular frame.

"Caleb." Dad's face lost some of the haggardness that seemed ever present. "Help me convince Willow that she needs to leave."

Caleb halted abruptly, as if Dad's words had surprised him. Then he finished closing the door and at the same time removed his hat. His murky, dark brown eyes searched the room until landing upon her. With one sweeping look, he took her in.

She didn't need to pretend with Caleb that she was okay. Even if she did, he'd see right through her acting. He always had. As her best friend for the past decade, he knew everything about her. Sometimes she felt as if he knew her even better than she knew herself.

One of his brows rose in a silent question, one that asked if she was okay.

The tightness in her lungs eased just a little, and she nodded. Now that he was here, everything would be all right. Caleb would make it all right. That's just the way he was.

"When Dad was out looking for employment today, he met Miss Rye." Willow lowered herself back to her chair, her legs suddenly weak. She wasn't sure if it was from hunger or worry or both.

Caleb's intense gaze scrutinized her as he waited as patiently as always for her to finish speaking.

Her dad nodded at her to continue, to go ahead and be the one to tell Caleb the news.

She drew in another breath, this one deeper into her lungs. "Apparently Miss Rye is organizing a transport for a select group of mill workers to sail to Vancouver Island where they'll be employed in domestic service."

Caleb's jaw flexed, bringing out the scar on his chin. A vein in his temple pulsed, highlighting the scar above his left eye. And his mouth flattened, revealing the tiny thin scar above his lip.

Because of his scars and his brawny build, Caleb held an intimidating air. He was tough and sullen and gruff to most people. But with her and her family, he was loyal and kind almost to a fault.

What did he think of the news? "Dad and Mum want me to go so that I can save up money for everyone else to emigrate."

Caleb remained silent, stoic. Only his jaw ticced again. Was he opposed? Would he figure out how she could stay?

She couldn't tell what he was thinking. She'd tried countless times over the years. But he kept his emotions locked away and rarely revealed them.

Dad stifled a cough then gave Caleb a pleading look. "Caleb and me, we talked about trying to find a way for Willow to emigrate to America or Canada just last week. Yeah?"

"You did?" Willow directed her question at Caleb.

He didn't respond, but that was answer enough.

"Why?" She couldn't keep the hurt from her tone.

Available now!

Connect With Sunrise

Thank you again for reading *A Convenient Heart*. We hope you enjoyed the story. If you did, would you be willing to do us a favor and leave a review? It doesn't have to be long—just a few words to help other readers know what they're getting. (But no spoilers! We don't want to wreck the fun!) Thank you again for reading!

We'd love to hear from you—not only about this story, but about any characters or stories you'd like to read in the future. Contact us at www.sunrisepublishing.com/contact.

We also have a monthly update that contains sneak peeks, reviews, upcoming releases, and fun stuff for our reader friends. Sign up at www.sunrisepublishing.com or scan our QR code.

Also by Lacy Williams

Christmas Bells and Wedding Vows (anthology)

Wagon Train Matches
A Trail So Lonesome
Trail of Secrets
A Trail Untamed
Wild Heart's Haven
A Rugged Beauty

Wind River Hearts series
Marrying Miss Marshal
Counterfeit Cowboy
Cowboy Pride
The Homesteader's Sweetheart
Courted by a Cowboy
Roping the Wrangler
Return of the Cowboy Doctor
The Wrangler's Inconvenient Wife
A Cowboy for Christmas
Her Convenient Cowboy
Her Cowboy Deputy
Catching the Cowgirl
The Cowboy's Honor
Winning the Schoolmarm
The Wrangler's Ready-Made Family
Christmas Homecoming
Heart of Gold

Made in United States
Cleveland, OH
30 June 2025

18165702R00139